A LOVE
BEYOND

KATE WELSH

Published by Steeple Hill Books™

STEEPLE HILL BOOKS

Steeple
Hill®

ISBN 0-373-87225-9

A LOVE BEYOND

Copyright © 2003 by Kate Welsh

Visit us at www.steeplehill.com

Printed in U.S.A.

F

"Cowboy, it's pretty obvious you wouldn't know one end of a horse from another."

"Nor do I really want to," Jim commented.

Crystal blinked in surprise but recovered quickly. "Good. Now that we have that settled, you can take yourself right back the way you came."

Jim couldn't fight a grin. This Amazon had a sharp tongue. Who would have thought?

"You think this is funny, slick?" she demanded.

"No. But you're misunderstanding why I'm here. I don't want to learn about horses. I just want to stay here and have a few questions answered. And the name's Jim, not slick."

With that, Jim was tempted to walk away. She was going to be more of a temptation than he'd thought. Staying here would be a problem for him, but deep inside he heard that still, small voice.

This was where he was supposed to be.

Books by Kate Welsh

Love Inspired

*For the Sake of
  Her Child* #39
Never Lie to an Angel #69
A Family for Christmas #83
Small-Town Dreams #100
Their Forever Love #120
*The Girl Next Door #156
*Silver Lining #173
*Mountain Laurel #187
*Her Perfect Match #196
Home to Safe Harbor #213
*A Love Beyond #218

Silhouette Special Edition

Substitute Daddy #1542

*Laurel Glen

KATE WELSH

is a two-time winner of Romance Writers of America's coveted Golden Heart Award and was a finalist for RWA's RITA® Award in 1999. Kate lives in Havertown, Pennsylvania, with her husband of over thirty years. When not at work in her home-office, creating stories and the characters that populate them, Kate fills her time in other creative outlets. There are few crafts she hasn't tried at least once or a sewing project that hasn't been a delicious temptation. Those ideas she can't resist grace her home or those of friends and family.

As a child she often lost herself in creating make-believe worlds and happily-ever-after tales. Kate turned back to creating happy endings when her husband challenged her to write down the stories in her head. With Jesus so much a part of her life, Kate found it natural to incorporate Him into her writing. Her goal is to entertain her readers with wholesome stories of the love between two people the Lord has brought together and to teach His truth while she entertains.

And He was withdrawn from them
about a stone's throw, and He knelt down and
prayed, saying, 'Father, if it is Your will, take this
cup away from Me; nevertheless not My will, but
Yours, be done.' Then an angel appeared to Him
from heaven, strengthening Him.

—*Luke* 22:41-43

For Martha,
for your steadfast support in all aspects of my life—
writing and personal. My gratitude and all my love.

Prologue

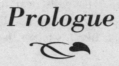

Jim Lovell felt as if he'd returned to the scene of the crime. His crime. Which was all wrong since he was a cop and he was supposed to serve and protect.

But he hadn't served or protected the owners of Laurel Glen. Instead he'd accused the wrong man, and nearly cost a nice guy his reputation and career, and a lovely woman her life. Cole Taggert, the man he'd falsely accused, had just asked for Jim's help and Jim hadn't been able to turn him down. So it looked as if Jim was on his way to Torrence, Colorado, the hometown of Laurel Glen's new foreman.

Now as Jim left Laurel Glen, he could only pray that helping the Taggerts would lighten his load of guilt. Flipping on his turn signal, Jim glided to a stop after passing under the iron entrance arch of the horse farm. Though deep in thought, he checked for oncoming traffic, then turned toward town and the state police barracks where he had to finish the week before starting his leave of absence.

He'd arranged for the leave to give himself time to examine his life and where it was going. He'd been a cop since he'd graduated from college and had been on the fast track to captain of a precinct in his hometown of Riverside, Pennsylvania. Then it had all gone south. He'd lost his fiancée in a drug shoot-out because she'd blown her undercover identity with a phone call to him. His guilt over that call had not lessened in all these years. Jim had hung on, though, telling himself that, like his father, he was born to be a cop.

Now he wasn't so sure.

Especially after last week when he'd almost been killed. Another detective had saved him by firing at a teenager bent on killing Jim. Once before, he'd been in the same kind of situation and had killed a gunman who was not much more than a boy. After that, he'd left inner-city law enforcement to take a job with the state police, but apparently hadn't left the incident behind.

Now he doubted he'd left any of his past behind.

So he was on his way west with nothing but the long road ahead and lots of time alone with the Lord. Maybe by the time he arrived in Colorado, Jim would know where to go from there.

Chapter One

"Sorry," Crystal Alton said a little breathlessly as she joined her friend Julia Winter at their usual table in Rusty's Place. "I've been running late all day. You won't believe this. I overslept."

"You never oversleep. Dawn breaks and you're awake."

Crystal shrugged, trying to look carefree. "I didn't sleep too well. It happened again last night."

Julia frowned. "What happened?"

"He kept me awake," Crystal replied, unable to bottle up the sigh in her lungs.

"Not more phone calls?" Julia blinked, worry shadowing her pale, blue eyes behind her wire-framed glasses.

"*Calls* is the operative word. Not one as usual. I lost count around six or seven. He called every half hour from ten until three. If I catch the little monster, he's going to be spending the rest of the summer mucking stalls till he drops."

"How would you catch him? Crystal, this is Torrence, not Denver. Sheriff King isn't…well…he isn't the best law enforcement has to offer."

Crystal chuckled at Julia's ability to make what should have been a scathing condemnation into only a minor criticism.

Rusty's latest waitress, Ralph Harris's girl, sauntered up to their table and dropped off silverware and water. She asked if they were ready to order. Regulars, they knew the menu and, since it was Wednesday, Julia ordered the chicken platter special. Crystal thought of ordering salad, but she hated salad. Not the taste but what it represented. Recently she'd decided trying to peel pounds off a body without an extra ounce of fat was not only useless, but stupid and dangerous. She gave an internal sigh. She was what she was, but the life of an Amazon was not always easy!

After ordering her favorite roast beef on rye with ketchup, Crystal grinned at her friend and waited. Seconds later, Rusty, who was cooking in the back, stuck his head out of the kitchen. He didn't disappoint her, shooting her a pithy comment. "You tell Crystal Alton if she wants ketchup polluting my prime beef, she can put it on herself."

Rusty Schreiber was a transplanted New Yorker who'd inherited Torrence's landmark diner from his great-aunt. He claimed to have come west to sell it, but once here, he'd found the town so deprived of good East Coast food he felt compelled to stay and save them all. It was Crystal's opinion that he'd taken one look at the town and had fallen in love with the simple life.

"You tell Rusty Schreiber," Crystal said, playing along, "that when I want his opinion on my eating habits, I'll hire him as a personal trainer. Not!"

"Crystal, what are you going to do about him?" Julia demanded. "You can't let this go on."

"Rusty's harmless. I think you should be nicer to him. He's kind of cute. Maybe he'd ask you out."

"I'm not talking about Rusty Schreiber and his acidic Eastern comments. Besides, I told you, I'm not interested in him. He…makes me nervous. You never know what he's going to do or say. But as I said, he's not what I'm talking about." Julia turned and glanced toward the kitchen. "Or maybe he is. Maybe he's the caller."

Crystal sputtered a laugh. "Rusty?"

Julia blushed. "Please don't make fun of me."

"It isn't Rusty. He just teases me the same way I do him. Don't take everything so seriously."

"Maybe it isn't Rusty but it's *someone*. You're no match for someone you can't see. This guy may just be bigger than you! Rusty Schreiber is, even if just a little. It doesn't matter how big and strong you are. This isn't the school playground anymore."

"Relax. I'm going to call Sheriff King. He can have the phone company trace the calls. That's what I told my prankster last night and that's exactly what I'm going to do. The calls started at ten and the last one was at three. I'm hoping he stops calling because I put a little fear into him. Since no kid could have been out at a pay phone at that hour, I've got the little monster right where he lives.''

Julia leaned forward. ''Don't trust Sheriff King. Call Jackson. He'll know what to do.''

Crystal didn't know if it was sleep deprivation or not, but at that moment she missed her brother so much, tears suddenly filled her eyes. ''I can't. He'll come home when he's ready.''

''But you need him so much right now. What did your father say about all those phone calls?''

''That I should take the phone off the hook. The calls were bothering him and he had an early day today.'' Crystal rolled her eyes. ''As if *I* didn't.''

''I'm sorry he wasn't sympathetic.'' Julia dabbed at her mouth with her napkin. ''But still, why didn't you just take the phone off the hook?''

Crystal shook her head. ''I was afraid Jackson might try to contact me. We used to talk late at night. And before you suggest it again, I won't drag him back here.''

''That's just because you two argued.'' Julia looked down at her hands. ''Crystal,'' she said, looking back up, her brows drawn together, ''Jackson's been your friend and confidant from the day you were born. You shouldn't have to go through this alone.''

Crystal sighed. Sometimes her friend could be a more than a little melodramatic. ''Will you stop. I'm not going *through* anything. It's just a few crank calls.''

Julia put her hand on Crystal's hand and squeezed. ''You don't know that. Think how terrible Jackson would feel if something happened to you.''

"Nothing is going to happen to me. Honestly, I wish I'd told you it was car trouble that made me late."

Her friend went on as if Crystal hadn't spoken. "He'll probably even feel bad when he finds out you've needed his moral support and felt you couldn't call on him. I bet you won't call him because you feel guilty for yelling at him before he left."

Crystal knew her friend didn't understand why Jackson had gone east and she wasn't at liberty to say. It was Jackson's news and only Jackson had the right to share it. "Believe me, that isn't the reason I won't call. This isn't the first disagreement we've had. Brothers and sisters disagree. They make up. We will, too." She prayed that was true. Not the part about making up. That she was sure of. But Crystal wasn't so sure about him still thinking of her as his sister now that he knew he was adopted.

"I feel terrible that I didn't realize the tension was so bad between him and your father," Julia said, her head bowed.

This was so typical of Julia to feel responsible for something that had nothing to do with her. "How were you supposed to know? And what could you have done if you had known?"

"Maybe he could have talked to me about his problems. You aren't exactly an impartial observer."

Crystal wouldn't hurt Julia for the world, but the fact was there was no way her brother would have discussed anything so personal with Julia. Her friend had had a crush on Jackson back in their high school days, and he hadn't been able to return her feelings.

To him, Julia would always be his sister's friend and no more, which was a shame. Jackson and Julia might be good for each other. She was so much nicer than the women he usually gravitated toward.

"What you don't understand is that this trip of his isn't only about his relationship with our father. It's about himself, too."

They were interrupted by the waitress, who arrived with their food. Crystal sat back for a moment and watched Julia. Sometimes she worried about Julia, who dressed beyond her years and always looked ready for a funeral. As far as Crystal knew, the only man her friend had ever been interested in had been Jackson and he hadn't even been a man at the time.

Crystal thought maybe Julia was just afraid to trust anyone after the way her parents had dumped her with her aunt Hanna when she was five. Her parents had excused themselves by telling everyone they wanted Julia to stay with her aunt so she could go to school and make friends while they earned a living on the rodeo circuit. Except her parents had never returned. When they were killed several years later, the adults in town gave a collective sigh of relief that the roller-coaster ride for Hanna and Julia Winter was finally over.

"Crystal. Yoo-hoo," Julia said, drawing Crystal from her thoughts.

She laughed. "Oh. Sorry. My brain was on a trip down memory lane. Remember what a big crush you had on my brother in high school?"

Julia blushed. "Memory lane is right. Now stop trying to change the subject. This thing with these calls could be serious. I've been thinking. What if it's more than a bored teenager trying to frighten you?''

Crystal blinked. ''What do you mean *more?*''

''What if the threats he makes are real? What if it's some kind of stalker?''

''A stalker? You've been watching too many police shows on TV. Stalkers are enamored of the victim. Who would be enamored of me? Besides, as you pointed out, this is Torrence, not Denver. Not a man in a fifty-mile radius of here has ever done more than slap me on the back or challenge me to a horse race.''

Julia shrugged. ''I worry about you. Especially now that you have to work with the cattle instead of in the ranch office. What if there's a stampede? Look at what almost happened when that bull wandered into the corral where you were working with that yearling.''

''And too many *Rawhide* reruns, too,'' Crystal said, grinning. ''Someone accidentally left a gate open. How could you have lived around livestock your whole life and not know that most bulls aren't that dangerous? I was fine. I *am* fine. I admit I hate the work. And add to that, I'm overworked right now. I liked spending the bulk of my days in my nice clean office, looking at my nice logical computer, doing the books and making stock market trades, but I'm in no danger now. I was raised on the Circle A. I had a horse ten years before I had a driver's license. Now relax and tell me what new books you're ordering for the fall so I can get my reading list in order.''

Crystal let her friend fill the rest of their time with library and town news. Talking about those annoying phone calls wasn't her idea of a pleasant luncheon topic. Julia finally wound down, and Crystal glanced at her watch. More time had passed than she'd thought.

"Jule, I have to run. We gabbed away an extra half hour. I had a meeting scheduled with Pastor Burns five minutes ago."

Wiping her mouth, Julia stood and collected her purse. "You go ahead. It's my turn to pay anyway. Remember, be careful."

"Yes, Mother," Crystal intoned as she hurried toward the door.

Minutes after arriving in Torrence, Jim Lovell parked his SUV in the parking lot of a diner called Rusty's Place. He climbed out of the vehicle he'd rented for the cross-country trip and took in the atmosphere.

Jack Alton's hometown was a quaint little place. And the terrain surrounding it was flat. Really flat. The plains stretched out in flowing gold giving everything a gilt-edged cast. It surprised Jim because back home in Pennsylvania that color meant fall, but it was only mid-August. *Amber waves* had a whole lot more meaning all of a sudden. And Torrence? Well, Torrence was small-town western America come to life.

The town had three churches along its tree-lined main street, appropriately named Main Street. All the businesses a town could need stood with architectures blending and complementing each other thanks to the common denominator of clapboard siding. It was a town that had clearly grown over time.

On one side of the street, Torrence had a town park that boasted a war memorial and a Victorian bandstand. The Torrence library and town hall were located on the opposite side of Main Street. Their architecture was also more formal than the rest of the town and, like the bandstand, built with a Victorian flair. The last building in the business district reminded him of a building straight out of an old Western movie. It was constructed of weathered gray clapboard and had an old-fashioned, raised wooden sidewalk and hitching posts at street level.

Past the square, a row of private homes lined Main Street, which flowed out of town. There was also a network of small streets intersecting Main Street where other houses were nestled in close to the sleepy little town.

As Jim reached out to open the diner's door, it swung inward and out of his reach. A flash of raven hair was all he saw before a woman barreled onto the sidewalk and into him. The impact of her solid body had him gasping for breath and backing up a few steps—literally and figuratively. Jim had always imagined that if angels turned out to be female, they would look much like this woman. Strong and sturdy with utterly perfect features.

Just like his Jessie had been. His heart twisted—ached—as he fought the pain of losing his fiancée, a pain that never seemed to go away.

"Oh, please excuse me," the woman said. "I've

been rushing and running behind on everything all day.''

She looked up then and he could only stare at the dark-haired woman still within the circle of his arms. Though his hands had landed close to her waist, he realized they were full of her flowing silky hair. A frown marred her smooth forehead above the most incredible eyes he'd ever seen. Like the rest of her, they were powerful and vibrant. Nearly as black as her hair but with wedges of blue and flecks of gold, they ensnared him with an inescapable force.

''Crystal, I thought you were in a hurry,'' a voice said from just behind her.

Crystal's startled gaze flickered and her magnetic field released its captive. ''Sorry,'' Jim said, though he didn't know what he'd apologized for.

At the same time, in a voice from his most secret fantasies, Crystal said, ''No. It was my fault. I wasn't watching where I was going.''

''Hey, no problem. Really,'' he told the raven-haired vision, who had packed such a wallop that he'd barely recovered enough breath to speak. And then she was gone, striding down the sidewalk and out of his life.

And that's the way it has to be. You know it, so quit whining.

As he watched her slide behind the wheel of a shiny little pickup, the regret for his long-ago vow had never felt stronger. Shaking his head, Jim took his own advice, putting her and his dissatisfaction aside. He was on a twofold mission and didn't have the energy to fight that particular internal battle once again. Though he and the Lord had gotten no further on his own personal issues during the drive west, it was time to put the question of his career aside for now and concentrate on the mysterious Jack Alton.

A quick survey of Rusty's Place told Jim this was exactly where he needed to start digging. A typical diner, it had a counter that helped separate the food prep areas from the tables and booths. Three waitresses bustled around serving customers, making coffee and shouting at some guy in the kitchen who, Jim assumed, was the cook. And the most important ingredient was there—an atmosphere of loose tongues among the town's people.

"Just find a seat, handsome," the middle-aged waitress shouted from behind the counter. "One of us will get to you ASAP."

Jim decided the waitress looked like his best bet for quick information so he headed for the lonely end of the counter. He straddled the stool and snatched up a menu.

A few minutes later the waitress approached with a cup in one hand and a coffeepot in the other. She lifted the pot and raised one painted-on eyebrow.

"Bless you," he said, and shot her a friendly smile. "I've been on the road since seven. The cup I started out with wore off a long, long time ago."

"I'm Janie West. Welcome to Torrence. So are you just passing through or looking for work, handsome?"

Now Jim really felt as if he'd stepped onto a Hollywood set. He'd heard Janie West's question at least once in nearly every Western movie he'd ever watched. With some difficulty, he didn't laugh and managed to maintain a neutral expression. And that wasn't easy because she looked and cracked her gum just like an actress who'd played a diner waitress on an old sitcom. Her hair was bottle red and twisted up in the same beauty-parlor style his mother had worn when he was a little kid. Janie even wore a plastic name pin fastened to her uniform backed by a lacy handkerchief.

Instead of laughing, which wouldn't earn him any points, he parroted his partially true cover story. He'd been writing a mystery on and off for two years. Most of his friends thought he was crazy to think he could be the next Wambaugh of the Christian book world.

"It's Jim Lovell, and actually I'm here to work but not looking for it. I'm a writer, or trying to be, so I have my work with me. I'm hoping to find some-where in town to stay so I can write and soak up the atmosphere. I'm working on a mystery set on a ranch and in a small western town, but I was raised in an eastern city. What I know about places like Torrence I've gotten from movies, and that just won't do in book-length fiction."

"Gee, Jim, we don't have any motels within thirty miles of here. Having a nice-lookin' fella like you around would've been nice."

Disappointed, he asked, "How about a B and B or someone who rents rooms?"

She shook her head. "Sorry, but... Hey. I've got an idea. Come here," she said, scooting out from be-hind the counter. She hurried toward the far end of the diner, and Jim followed as ordered.

He was game for anything that got people comfortable with him and brought him closer to getting the answers Cole Taggert wanted. Answers he was determined to get, but carefully. It wouldn't do to have people grow suspicious of him or begin to speculate that he was investigating Jack Alton. The one thing he didn't want to do was damage a good man's reputation, as he had done with Cole. It was altogether possible that Alton was exactly what he said he was. Similar looks to the Taggert family proved nothing even though Jim was suspicious.

Waitress Janie stopped at a bulletin board mounted between the rest room doors and rooted around the surface, lifting notices and pinning them back on. Finally she tore one off. "Here it is. There's a cabin for rent on the biggest ranch in the area. I don't know why he'd want to rent it out, but it could be he just has a good mad on. He sure doesn't need the money. This'll be perfect for you if he hasn't changed his mind."

She handed him the hand-printed card. "'For rent. Two-bedroom cabin. Inquire—Circle A. See Evan or Crystal Alton,'" Jim read aloud. He couldn't believe his luck. But then it wasn't luck at all, was it?

Thank you, Lord. This makes life a whole lot easier.

"So what's this Alton guy so mad about?" Jim asked, still pretending to consider the idea of the cabin minutes after he gave Janie his lunch order.

"Mad? Oh, Evan's son, Jackson, had just moved into the cabin when he took off all of a sudden. Most of us knew there was tension between the two of them. Jackson's best friend, Seth Stewart, said that's why Jackson moved into the cabin. Since he'd just furnished the place so nice and all, we were shocked. Didn't think that boy would ever give up on the Circle A. But he just up and disappeared one day.''

"Surely his family knows where he is," Jim said, meanwhile filing away an important piece of information. Alton's given name was Jackson and it seemed everyone called him that and not Jack, the name used by Laurel Glen's new foreman. Significant but hardly damning information. Seth Stewart—one of Alton's so-called references—was his friend, not his employer. And apparently Alton had always worked with Evan Alton, his father, at their own ranch. Curiouser and curiouser.

The waitress shrugged in answer to his quasi-question about the Alton family. "Well, I'd guess they have some idea where he is since Crystal doesn't seem worried—just a little sad. She and Jackson are best friends, not just brother and sister. When anyone asks, she just says he'll come home when he's good and ready."

What was the matter with him, he wondered as the name clicked in his brain. Crystal. That was the angel's name. "Crystal," he said, and took the card out of his pocket. "Wasn't that the name of the woman leaving as I came in?"

"Don't know, but she was just in here with Julia Winter."

"About six foot tall. Long black hair. Incredible eyes."

"That'd be Crystal." Janie waggled those painted-on eyebrows. "It'd be nice to see a guy interested in

.her for a change. Maybe this cabin'll work out even better for you than you thought.''

Not in Jim's estimation. Crystal Alton was more temptation than he needed. But he had no choice if he was going to stay in Torrence, and staying was imperative. Nope, the cabin no longer felt like such a good deal at all.

Chapter Two

Jim followed the waitress's directions and was soon driving along the Circle A's dusty private road. The first building he came to was a long, low house resembling many "ranch"-style houses back East except for the deeply pitched roof. It was the setting—squared-off log construction and burnt red tile roof of nearly the same color as the stain on the logs—that made the house unique to him. Accented with specimen trees planted in big terra-cotta pots, a matching red stone patio surrounded the entire house. Towering elms almost completely encircled the house, giving the structure a nestled-in feel that Jim really liked. Though large and spread out, the house looked welcoming and comfortable.

In the distance, Jim saw more low buildings and attached corrals, all painted the same subdued red, perhaps even a bit faded from the strong sunlight. Several vehicles sat beyond the house in a circular parking area, so he pulled his car to a stop there and got out.

It took a few minutes on foot to reach the first corral where several cowboys stood in a circle, listening to someone in the center giving instructions. Jim hung back and when the group broke up, he realized the person in the center was none other than the raven-haired beauty with the fascinating eyes. Her dark hair had since been braided and tamed into a thick rope that hung nearly to her waist.

Crystal Alton was indeed a temptation and for more than just her looks. There was her height and substantial build, which were so much like Jessie's. Jim had always been drawn to tall women with a healthy-looking physique. Even in his teens he'd found it disconcerting to spend time with a delicate flower a good hug would break in half. How did big men spend their lives with women who were half their size?

"Oh, please, tell me you aren't here about the wrangler job," Crystal Alton all but growled as she snatched a white woven cowboy hat off the fence post.

Jim blinked back to the present, trying to recover from the lost-feeling thoughts that Jessie always left him with. He opened his mouth to tell Crystal Alton that he wouldn't take a job working with horses for anything, but she didn't wait for his denial.

"Come on, cowboy," she said, her voice thick with sarcasm. "I'm not that dumb. Even that accent of yours screams eastern city. You aren't getting days' worth of free room and board out of me while you pretend you're used to Western tack. It's pretty obvious you wouldn't know one end of a horse from another."

"Nor do I really want to," Jim commented.

Crystal Alton blinked in surprise, but recovered quickly. "Good. Now that we have that settled you can just take yourself right back the way you came. I don't have time for games."

Jim couldn't fight a grin. His apologetic angel had a sharp tongue. Who'd have thought?

"You think this is funny, slick?" she demanded.

"No. Not at all. But you misunderstand why I'm here."

"I doubt it. This isn't a trainee job."

"But I told you, I don't want to learn about horses. Not really. I just want to stay here and have a few questions answered. And by the way, the name's Jim Lovell, not 'slick.'"

Her volume increased. "Ask questions? Stay here? Does this look like a library or a hotel?"

Jim was tempted to retreat. She was going to be more of a temptation than he'd thought. Staying here would be a problem for him, but deep inside he heard that still, small voice. This was where he was supposed to be. Jim fished out the card he'd gotten from Rusty's bulletin board and read, "'For rent. Two bedroom cabin. Inquire—Circle A. See Evan or Crystal Alton.' You are Crystal Alton, right? Janie at the diner gave this to me and the directions."

"Let me see that!" she demanded, and snatched it from him to read for herself. Her eyes blazed like twin flames when she looked back up. "I didn't think he'd do it. I'll be back,'' she said and stalked away with a furious but graceful long-legged stride.

Crystal Alton was some woman.

The kind of woman he'd always admired but the kind that, according to both his sister and his late fiancée, Jessie, often went unappreciated. When he'd thought of spending a lifetime with a woman, this had been the kind of woman he'd gravitated toward. But that had been before Jim learned that strong substantial women weren't any less breakable than all the others. When he lost Jessie, he'd lost most of himself with her.

And inside, that part of his heart was still dead.

Jim would never forget the moment it had flickered and died. The call had come when he'd been in his car. *"Officers down."* A message a police officer dreaded.

An undercover narcotics operation had gone bad. Really bad. Jessie Cushing—his Jessie—and his best friend, Greg Peterson, had been shot. Jim had made it to the scene even before the ambulances. Other cops had tried to stop him, but he'd fought them off. And he'd found Greg, leaning against a Dumpster, holding Jessie. With tears streaming down his pale cheeks Greg had looked up from that trash-strewn street and Jim had seen his friend's abject sorrow. He'd known she was gone and in that instant Jim's insides had gone hollow.

In the hours that followed, as doctors tried valiantly and finally succeeded in saving Greg, Jim had sat in the hospital, trying to find the part of him Jessie had occupied. But as one after another of his fellow officers had come to pay condolences and offer support, he'd realized that part of him was close to death, too.

And he'd let it die.

It had hurt less that way. Still did.

Jim pretended to everyone that he was the same, that he'd moved on. But that didn't make it true. Inside, where feelings and love were supposed to live, he was empty and pretty determined to stay that way. At least if he had anything to say about it, he would. Because having that place filled was too risky. He would never again chance feeling that kind of crushing grief.

Crystal stared at her father. "I can't believe you did this."

"And I can't believe I raised a son who'd desert the ranch I built for him to go traipsing across the country in search of a woman who didn't want him in the first place. The cabin's up for rent. End of discussion."

Crystal stared at her father. He was a handsome, brooding man who worked too hard and grieved too hard and had done both for way too long. When she was ten and Jackson was twelve, Crystal used to think if they ran away, Evan Alton would finally notice them. But she'd never tried running away and neither had Jackson.

Until June, when Jackson had effectively run away to search for his roots.

Of course, other than making his father angry, Jackson's quest hadn't seemed to affect their father emotionally. He hadn't seemed hurt nor did he seem to miss his son in any way other than to complain about the increased workload Jackson's absence caused. Some things never changed. She guessed even at ten she'd understood that.

"Why are you doing this?" she demanded.

His gaze never flickered. "Because I can. Does this guy seem like a decent sort?"

"I suppose he seems decent but—"

"Then tell him the rent's six hundred a month."

"And what if Jackson comes home tomorrow?"

"Then your brother can stay in the big house where he grew up. I had Anna move his clothes and personal things back to his room the day I hung the notice."

"You had no right. And remember this, if he turns right around and leaves again, it's on your head."

Crystal stalked back to Jim Lovell. "You can move in. Six hundred a month. No smoking. No drunkenness. No female overnighters. You break any of my rules, you'll find your bags packed and on the hood of your car."

"Fine. Since I don't drink or smoke and don't plan to ever get married, that shouldn't be much of a problem."

Crystal took in the significance of his premodern-age remark and dismissed it as his just trying to make a good impression. "Don't try so hard, slick," she told him, then grimly led the way to the cabin—the same one her brother had lived in before he'd realized that until he met his biological mother he'd have no peace.

Jackson had tried to stay, though. From the end of March till the beginning of June he'd known there

was a position open at Laurel Glen and, still, he'd
stayed at the Circle A, trying to forget the years of
lies that lay between him and their father. But the
help-wanted ad had continued to appear in Jackson's
favorite equestrian magazine till he'd given in and
called. He'd decided the Lord must be sending him
to Laurel Glen.

And the rest was history, Crystal thought as she
unlocked the cabin door and entered the room with
Jim Lovell close on her heels. She and Jackson had
fixed it up together. It was a restful place with little
touches of color here and there. There was a leashed
power in her brother that many missed, but it lingered
in the big, soft, crimson pillows he'd tossed on the
burnt umber leather sofa. A matching throw rug lay
across the overstuffed chair and ottoman, which sat
angled toward the stone fireplace.

Jackson had bought a couple of smaller Reming-
tons, which he'd displayed on a table between two
windows about four feet behind the sofa. A Bob
DeJulio watercolor landscape hung between the windows. The master bedroom entrance was on the ad-
joining wall and the room shared the fireplace from
the other side. The kitchen and dining area were on
the opposite side of the big open room, and a bath
and smaller bedroom were located at the rear of the
cabin.

Crystal and her brother had fun working together,
but for the first time in her memory, Jackson had been
restless with an underlying sadness—until he'd made
his decision to seek out his birth mother. And even

then the sadness had remained. It was as if he'd lost something. Crystal was very afraid he'd lost himself.

"This is all my brother's," she said, feeling protective and possessive of the essence Jackson left behind. "Take care of it. The master bedroom's back there," she said, pointing past the sofa and end table. "It has a private bath. Second bedroom's there to the right, though you won't need it. It's set up as a guest room, but does dual duty as a private office for Jackson."

She turned then and saw surprise on his face. "What were you expecting? A line shack?"

"The notice said cabin. I was thinking something less civilized. This is terrific. So where's your brother?"

She frowned. It was too sore a subject right then. And Jim Lovell wearing brand new, off-the-shelf Western wear, was such a commanding presence standing there in Jackson's little home. "That's really none of your business. He's obviously not here or you wouldn't be."

"Look, I didn't mean to intrude. It was just an idle question. I don't know what I did to get on your bad side. I apologized for our little collision at the diner and, at least back then, you seemed to blame yourself."

Crystal closed her eyes. *What's the matter with me, Lord?*

She looked up at the big Nordic-looking guy with confusion written on his handsome face and felt mean and petty. This wasn't his fault. Neither was her exhaustion his fault. Nor her frustration with the job.

Nor her sense of loss when she looked around at what should have been Jackson's happy little sanctuary. None of it.

"I'm sorry. I'm so sorry. This may not have been the worst day of my life, but it ranks up there in the top ten right next to falling out of the hayloft and breaking my arm on the first day of summer vacation."

"I hear you. I did the same thing. Of course, my tumble was off the fire escape into the back alley, but the result was probably the same. No swimming. No bike riding. Bummer. Sorry if my arrival caused problems, but like I said, the waitress at the diner gave me the notice. I was looking for a place like this to write, so—"

"Write?" She stared at him. "You're a writer?" This mountain of a man, who exuded danger with every move, expected her to believe he supported himself by sitting at a computer all day? With those muscles?

"It's a mystery set on a ranch and near a small town," he replied.

He had an open, honest face, but she just didn't believe him. It didn't fit with the catlike grace of his walk. "What's it about?" she asked, hoping to catch him up. Was he a reporter trying to get the inside story on her successful, reclusive father?

"About?" Lovell asked.

"The book you're writing?" Didn't writers like to talk about their current projects? She would have thought they did.

His heavily lashed, big, brown eyes, which were

rather incongruous with all that Nordic coloring and size, widened. "Oh. That." He hesitated seeming nervous and unsure of himself—a condition she doubted he was used to. Then he nodded enthusiastically. "Well, okay. If you're interested. Most people aren't. Most people think I'm crazy. It's set around a ranch and a small town. That's why staying here is so perfect."

She crossed her arms. "You said that already. What's the mystery? Who are the main characters?"

"It's about a woman who lives on a ranch with her parents. She grew up with all the people in town. That's why I decided it had to be a small town...so the sheriff can't figure out who the perp is."

Crystal frowned. "Perp? As in perpetrator?"

Jim Lovell nodded. "He's stalking her."

Crystal could feel the blood drain from her head. She backed away. "It's about a stalker?" she asked. Could Julia be right? Could the calls be from a stalker? Could it be Jim Lovell behind the calls, and not a kid with mischief on his mind?

Lovell was frowning at her, looking concerned. But weren't some criminals good actors? They disarmed their victims with their charm, then moved in for the kill.

"Are you all right?" he asked.

"Fine." She took another backward step toward the door. "I'm just busy. I have to go now. The key's in the door. Remember the rules."

Crystal turned and fled. She needed to check on the volume of water available in the far northwestern corner of the property, so she saddled Lady and headed out of the corral. Riding Lady, a surefooted quarter horse her brother bought her for Christmas five years ago, usually brought her a measure of peace and contentment. Ten minutes later, as she rode toward Half-pint Spring, she felt the scenery and sunshine of God's pretty, summer day seep into her and calm her jitters.

Finally able to think more clearly, Crystal was appalled by her own behavior. This afternoon, she hadn't been willing to accept Julia's outlandish theory of a stalker, and now she'd run nearly full-throttle from what was possibly a very nice man. And even before that, she'd treated Jim Lovell with an appalling disdain and lack of civility.

Pressure, annoyance, lack of sleep were just no excuse.

She owed him another great, big apology. Crystal pulled her watch out of the pocket of her jeans and popped the cover. If all went well, she'd have time to offer that apology when she got back to the ranch compound.

Sounds of distress reached Crystal and she moved Lady into a canter, estimating them as coming from nearly a quarter mile away off. When she got to Half-pint Spring she mentally thanked her favorite philosopher of late, a certain legendary Mr. Murphy, for all his dire warnings. Her bad day had just gotten worse. But then, when she looked at the poor bedraggled calf who'd gotten himself stuck up to his belly in mud—all five hundred pounds of him—Crystal figured she wasn't the only one having a bad day.

Chapter Three

Jim watched Crystal Alton ride into the dusty corral not long after sunset. It was still light enough to see she was muddy and uncomfortable as she led her horse toward the barn. When she turned it over to Tomas, the little guy who cared for the horses, she clapped him on the back as if in gratitude. The set of her shoulders and the uneven determinedness of her gait as she struck out in the direction of the house, told of someone who was exhausted after a really aggravating day. Since he'd been part of that aggravation, Jim decided it would be really smart if he stayed safely where he was. There was plenty of time to pump her for information about her missing brother once her mood had improved.

Besides, with today having provided more questions than answers about the man, Jim had a lot to think about already. It turned out that none of the men on the Circle A seemed to know where Jackson Alton was. They all said the same thing: One day Jackson and his shiny new pickup truck had just disappeared.

Unlike Crystal Alton's, though, Jim's day hadn't been completely bad. He'd learned a few more things. From Tomas, he'd found out that Jackson and his father had argued in the barn late the night before the younger Alton disappeared. The most significant piece of information Jim had turned up so far was that it was a mistake to discount the name discrepancy between Jackson and Jack. Everyone, absolutely everyone, since he'd hit Torrence, called the man Jackson and not Jack.

He'd also managed to meet Evan Alton. He was a tall, commanding man with iron-gray hair and eyes and a youthful face despite the lines carved around his eyes from years of squinting in the sunlight. Jim imagined women would find him attractive, as was true of his son, but that son looked nothing like his father. And a quickly snapped answer to one carefully worded question was all it had taken for Jim to get the message—it was not a good idea to even mention Jackson to his father.

Some might see Alton's reaction as angry, but as a cop, Jim had become a careful observer of human emotions, and the man was deeply hurt by his son's seemingly out-of-character disappearance.

And just as appearances could be deceiving, sometimes the absence of them could carry great meaning. Jim couldn't ignore the lack of a resemblance between father and son when Jackson Alton looked like part of the Taggert clan. Cole's theory was that the younger Alton was adopted and actually a Taggert.

A new disturbing idea arose, but was no less far-fetched. Was the man he'd been sent to investigate actually Jackson Alton, or had the real Alton met with foul play only to have his identity stolen by the new foreman at Laurel Glen? Was someone here bent on mischief? Had the scion of the Circle A actually disappeared?

Two theories existed, and the confirmation of either would set one of the families on its ear. Jim thought it was a supreme twist of irony that the answer would be found in a picture of Jackson's face—the face that had begun all the suspicion in the first place.

At ten the next morning, Jim was on his way to Torrence's public library where he planned to explore old newspaper clippings. His plan was simple. The son of the wealthiest man in a town the size of Torrence had to have wound up with his picture in the paper at least once. Failing that, he'd find out if, like many small-town libraries, this one kept a copy of old high school yearbooks in the town history section.

"Well, hello, handsome," Janie West called out as he approached the steps of the library.

"Morning," he said, deciding to fish for a little more town gossip. "Thanks again for the tip about the cabin. I may never want to leave. The Altons' idea of a cabin and mine are pretty different. I can't imagine Jackson Alton leaving such a beautiful place behind."

Unfortunately, her only reply was a noncommittal shrug.

"I'm using his bed and I don't even have a clue

what he looks like. I'm kind of curious about the guy. The curse of a writer's mind, I guess. I always seem to need the whole story."

"He's good-looking. Real good-looking." She winked. "'Bout like you, handsome."

Jim grinned to cover his discomfort with her brash familiarity and pointed at the steps. "Well, research calls. I work for a real slave driver."

She seemed to miss his joke and checked her watch. She sighed. "Me, too. Look's like break time's over. You take care. Hear?"

"You, too," he said and vaulted up the stairs to the front doors.

Once inside, he took a deep breath then moved toward the information desk, ready for a little more acting. The woman who was sorting through mail looked up from her task. "May I help you?"

Jim recognized her as the same woman who'd been with Crystal at Rusty's Place yesterday. "I wondered if you archived old newspapers here," he asked, hoping his request didn't seem odd to her.

"Oh, certainly. This way," she said, and moved off to the left into an old-fashioned glassed-in office. "What is it you were looking for?"

"I'm a writer doing research on ranches and the small towns around them."

"Nothing will give you the flavor of a small town faster than its old editions. Good luck. Hope you find what you're looking for."

Jim nodded and started his hunt. He spent several hours there before dispelling his theory with a picture of the winner of a local rodeo several years earlier.

Jack and Jackson were one and the same. It seemed the Taggert family might once again be headed for a rough ride.

He noticed the editions went back to about the time of Jackson Alton's birth so he kept digging. After more searching he found a birth announcement and notice of the filing of a birth certificate.

That discovery unfortunately led to more questions. The names didn't match. Laurel Glen's new foreman was originally named Wade J. Alton—he assumed the *J* stood for Jackson—but not three weeks later an announcement of the birth of Martha and Evan Alton's son was in the society section. There he was called Jackson. It didn't prove the man had been adopted by the Altons, but it certainly left the possibility wide open.

At nearly one o'clock, Jim left the library and headed for the parking lot, deep in thought. A truck pulled in next to his, but he didn't pay it any mind as he unlocked the door of his SUV. He was too busy trying to decide if it was time to call Cole. He didn't really have any definitive answers, though. Just one less question and no proof to the other answer.

"You look like a man with a lot on your mind," a familiar female voice said.

Jim turned to look toward her across the hood of his SUV. Crystal Alton smiled at him. It was a smile that beckoned him in a way so elemental, he found himself grinning back. "Threads. You think you have a mystery solved and another one pops up to scramble your thinking," he explained.

She tilted her head to the side, considering him.

Her thick, silky-looking braid fell over her shoulder and turned the masculine-looking, well-worn, chambray shirt feminine in the blink of an eye.

"Being a writer must be rewarding. And you get to set your own hours."

"It looks as if you do the same thing," he commented, trying to hang on to the threads of the conversation.

She shook her head. "No. In my case, the cattle and my father do. I had obligations on Wednesdays before I agreed to take over as foreman. Wednesdays I have lunch with my friend Julia, and in the afternoon I work at church. I'm only here today because the work at church got shifted to today this week because we're getting ready for Summer Fun Days. It's a carnival and craft fair. You know, it might be good for you to come along. You'd have the chance to get a feel for the people and the way they live. There are both ranchers and townspeople involved."

She'd caught him completely off guard. "I thought you hated me."

Crystal shook her head. "Did I mention what a bad day I'd had?"

Jim nodded. "And you apologized. Then we were talking and suddenly you bolted like the house was on fire. It was you who asked about the book. I didn't mean to bore you."

"It was time I got going. And it was a good thing I did. I found a calf, a nice five hundred pounder, stuck in a dried-up watering hole. It took a while to get the poor dumb little guy out of the mud."

"Five hundred pounds doesn't sound little to me."

She smiled. "You really do need this research trip. By October when we ship our calves, they'll go between six and six hundred fifty pounds."

"Wow. I guess it's a good thing it wasn't fully grown."

She chuckled. "You have no idea. So? Are you interested in coming along to the church?"

Her smile lifted his spirits and Jim laughed. "Yeah. Why should this trip be any different than my real life? My best friend's a pastor and he ropes me into more building projects than you can imagine. He even got me involved in helping convert a barn into a church for a friend of his."

"Great. And don't worry. This isn't anything as grandiose. It's just knocking together some booths. The ones we've been using for the last few years are about done in."

Almost as an afterthought, Jim remembered that this would give him the opportunity to ask more questions about her brother.

But somehow, during the afternoon of camaraderie the subject of her brother never came up.

He did notice one peculiar thing about the way all the men—and the women, too—treated Crystal. And that was like she was a guy. Several times women having trouble with mechanical or strength issues called to her for help rather than one of the men. Even a couple of guys had done it. And all the men had called her Cris. So much less feminine a name than her pretty face and curvy body deserved. He shouldn't have been surprised after the way he'd seen Jessie and his sister, Joy treated, but he was. It just proved what he'd once told his sister: Most men were blind fools.

Jim hadn't been able to keep his thoughts or his eyes off Crystal all afternoon, and drills, saws, hammers or nails hadn't had a thing to do with his difficulty. The memory of those few seconds of her in his arms made it difficult. He didn't know how he'd do it, but before he left Torrence, Crystal would see herself as the beautiful woman she was.

It was nearly seven when they all knocked off, having accomplished quite a bit of work. All the workers thanked Jim profusely for his help as they separated at their cars.

"You feel like stopping for dinner?" he asked Crystal.

"Good idea. My father left this morning for meetings in Denver so I'd be eating alone. I gave our housekeeper the day off. Since I'm not the best cook in the world, I haven't been looking forward to eating my own cooking."

"Rusty's? Or is there another place to eat?" he asked.

Crystal shook her head. "Rusty's is it unless you feel like a fifty-mile drive."

"Not really. I still haven't recovered from the trip here. Let's take your pickup. You can drop me back here after we eat."

"Great," she said, and motioned to the passenger side of her truck. Once they'd both climbed in, Crystal continued their conversation. "You were such a big help today," she told him with a sweet smile. "You weren't kidding about knowing your way around construction. Did you really help convert a barn into a church?''

"Yeah. It's called the Tabernacle. I got out there every weekend I was off while it was being converted. It got me out of the city and it was terrific to be part of something so solid and long lasting. It was even better because it was for the Lord.''

"I apologize for doubting you at first.''

"Huh?''

"No smoking, drinking, women,'' she hinted.

"You thought I was just trying to make a good impression on my pretty landlady.''

"The thought crossed my mind.'' Her smile was a little sheepish and she blushed—at what he was afraid was an infrequent compliment.

Blind fools is right!

"Believe me, it was an unconventional answer considering some of the men who drift through here.''

"That's okay. It's an unconventional answer anywhere these days. Once, it would have been for me.''

"You weren't raised a Christian?'' Crystal asked as she parked in front of Rusty's Place.

Jim noticed she didn't lock the pickup when she got out. He shrugged. Probably par for the course around there. Who was going to steal a vehicle when everyone knew what everyone else drove?

"I wasn't raised in any church,'' he explained when he joined her on the sidewalk in front of the diner. "Remember that friend of mine I mentioned who's a pastor? If it hadn't been for his family, the name of Jesus would have been nothing more than a curse to me. All his talk of God was like water on stone, though. He finally wore down my resistance one day.

"Greg preached his first message in the new church and aimed it straight at me. He probably figured that was going to be his only formal shot at me. He had me trapped in the front row for an hour and he didn't waste the opportunity. I'd been pretty hostile about God till then."

"I've never met anyone who made that kind of conscious decision in their adult years," Crystal said. "My brother and I did it the way we did everything else. Together. He was twelve and I was ten. Our old pastor, Pastor Wayne, got to us with the idea of a Father who'd always love us. It appealed to us both."

Why had Cole left out the fact that Jack Alton was a Christian? He either didn't know or thought it didn't matter. But it did. At least it did to Jim. It made his job there even more difficult. Jackson Alton's faith meant there was less chance he was up to no good and made it all the more important for Jim to take care not to do any harm to the man's reputation.

"Jim? Is something wrong?"

Jim heard the puzzled tone in Crystal's voice even before her question registered. He looked around. While he'd been deep in thought, he'd unconsciously followed her inside and had actually slid across from her in a booth.

"Sorry, once in a while I get so deep into my thoughts, the rest of humanity just fades away." He smiled, but knew he probably looked as stiff as he felt. That was what had happened that day a month ago when the kid pulled the gun on him. The sound of gunfire had snapped him out of it then the way Crystal's voice had this time and earlier in the day. What was wrong with him?

"So what's good to eat?" he asked, hoping to distract her.

Crystal waved to Jim as she pulled away from Rusty's an hour later. He was such a nice guy. And a real hunk. Being with him did funny things to her insides and her mind. Around him she actually felt, if not delicate, at least feminine. He didn't treat her the way other guys did, either. She was pretty sure he'd never punch her shoulder, slap her on the back or put a skunk in her truck.

And he called her Crystal even after hearing the men called her Cris all day. He'd opened the diner door for her. Going in and coming out. And had paid for her dinner. It had felt almost like a date.

Her first.

After years of being just one of the guys, she understood what all the hoopla was about. And it was wonderful. He was such a hunk! Tomorrow she'd call Julia and—

Thunk!

No warning at all. Just a smack from the side and the wheel spun out of her hand. A flash of light color. The scream of metal. Her head smashing into the window next to her. And a smothering blackness that smacked into her face, engulfing her in its choking grip.

"How on earth did I get such a headache?" Crystal muttered aloud. On hearing her own voice, she forced her gritty eyes open. But nothing changed. Everything was still black. Her head still ached. Her shoulder was on fire. She put her fingertips on her temple and found something sticky trickling down her face.

Okay, Crystal, think. Where are you? she demanded, forcing herself to think.

She reached in front of her and her hands encountered the steering wheel of her truck, but there was something heavy blanketing it—and her.

The air bag!

An impact at her side. The sound of metal against metal. Losing control as the wheel spun out of her hands. The road dropping out from under her. A deep thud she'd felt at her center. The screech and crunch of tortured metal. It all came rushing back in one terrifying second.

Quickly Crystal undid her seat belt and tried to open her door, but it was wedged shut. She slid across the seat, encountering her purse. Dragging it with her, she pushed the passenger door open. The interior light stabbed at the back of her eyes and she fled the pickup with its punishing glare.

She slid to the ground and kept on going till her bottom hit the ground when her legs refused to hold her upright.

Her own weakness scared her.

The car that had hit her hadn't stopped to offer aid. That scared her even more.

"I need help," she muttered, and reached in her purse into the center zipper compartment for her cell phone, but it wasn't there. She always kept it right there. Something crinkled in her hand as she blindly hunted.

Forcing herself to her feet, Crystal tilted the purse toward the light. She found no cell phone. Puzzled, she open up the piece of paper she'd found.

Remember, I'm watching you. I can have you with me whenever I choose. Reject me again and you'll die. This was a warning just like last time. Did you really think that corral was left open by accident?

Crystal's heartbeat, already racing, picked up its furious pace. The evil words had been cut from glossy magazine paper and pasted on the page. She started to shake and sank down next to the truck again, holding on to the running board for dear life. The open gate in Gentleman Jake's corral had been a minor danger. Now he'd run her off the road. More dangerous still. Worrywart Julia had been right. It really was a stalker. And he wasn't only escalating his contact with her. He'd gone on the attack! What would he do next?

She tried to think if she'd seen anyone suspicious at the church, but admitted she hadn't. Everyone there had belonged there. Then the doubts rolled in. Who among her neighbors and friends could it be?

Crystal didn't have time to consider answers to those questions when headlights and the sound of a car cut through the darkness. And a new question blasted through her aching head.

Was it friend or foe coming up the road toward her? And how could she tell the difference?

A scant minute later she heard her name being called. The voice was frantic. It was Jim Lovell's voice. The voice of a stranger who said he was writing a book about a stalker.

And all of a sudden her questions had one clear possible answer.

Jim Lovell?

Chapter Four

"Crystal," Jim shouted again. "Are you all right?"

He really did sound worried, she thought. But still she didn't answer. Instead she crawled around the front of the pickup and into the tall grass. She peered out from the dense golden cover as he scrambled up the other side of the shallow drainage ditch in the light of his headlights.

It was a miracle, she thought absently, that her truck hadn't turned over there but had continued on before hitting the tree. How that happened was lost to her, though. At that moment, all she knew were confusion and pain.

And more fear than she ever remembered.

Jim once again called out to her and she lost sight of him on the other side of the pickup. That's when she decided. She broke cover and sprinted for his still-running SUV.

"Halt!" he shouted with such command that she did as ordered.

Then she looked back to see him barreling after her and fear freed her. Crystal took off again, slid down the incline of the ditch and clambered up the other side on all fours. She scrambled to her feet with the aid of the SUV's bumper, but got no farther.

He grabbed her just as the blinding light from the high beams knifed through her head. Screaming, she twisted toward him, ready to use one of the self-defense moves her brother had drilled into her in her teen years.

But he'd already let go, stepping back with his arms spread and a palms-out gesture that told her she was in charge. It was only then that she realized his hold hadn't been rough or threatening—just firm and powerful.

Crystal backed up a few steps, staring at him. He took a step toward her, reaching out with one arm half extended. She backed up.

He froze. "You're hurt," he said, his tone the same one she'd heard her brother use on a wild mustang he was trying to gentle. In the glare of the headlights, Jim's eyes were so calm and reassuring that they were nearly hypnotizing. "You need help," he went on, not moving an inch toward her. "Crystal? Do you understand what I'm saying?"

Still undecided, she cut her eyes toward the SUV. Her heart tripped. It was red! Bright. Shining. Beautiful. Red. Not white. Not silver. Red.

How could she have forgotten? How could she have convinced herself he was even a possible suspect? The calls had begun weeks before his arrival, as had the incident with Gentleman Jake.

Her legs went rubbery once again and she would have fallen had Jim not been there gathering her close. Tears burned her eyes and throat and rolled down her cheeks. And sounds—sounds of a frightened animal—broke loose from her throat.

"Take it easy. Take it easy. You're safe," he murmured.

With the soothing sound of his voice and the force of his easy hold surrounding her, Crystal realized that was exactly how she felt. Safe.

"Come here. Come on. Let's get you sitting down," he suggested as he guided her to the wide running board of the big red SUV. Then he pulled a handkerchief from his back pocket and pressed it to her head. She flinched, but he didn't let up the pressure. "Can you hold this?" he asked after a minute or two.

"I think so," she answered, reaching up with shaking hands to the handkerchief. He took her hand and pressed it onto where he'd been applying pressure. She felt her hand quaking in his. She was trembling the way a frightened bird she'd once rescued during a severe windstorm had.

"Try to calm down," Jim said quietly, then stretched to reach through the open driver's window. She heard him rummage in the door for something, then he knelt in front of her and flipped a small pinpoint light into her right eye then her left.

She gasped as pain shot through her head.

"Sorry. Your pupils are reacting a little slowly."

He took over the pressure on the head wound and told her to squeeze his fingers with each of her hands, then he had her push against his hand. "I think you have a concussion, but I don't think it's a bad one or I'd take you to the hospital and forget the crime scene."

How had he guessed it was a crime scene? she wondered as he let up on the pressure he had on the cut.

"It stopped. That's good," he told her, then took her wrist while staring at the lit face of his watch. "Your pulse is still racing. Take some deep breaths. Try to calm down. It's over. You're going to be fine and you're safe."

"For now," she said, and looked up at him trying to gauge his reaction. "It wasn't an accident. He didn't stop. He came out of nowhere, smashed into me then he kept going."

His grin was slightly teasing but still tender. "Honey, that happens all the time in the big city. It's called a hit-and-run. Did you call the sheriff?"

"No. Somebody took it," she said, feeling slow-witted and still a little dazed. What was wrong with her?

"Took it? Took what?" Jim asked, worry evident in his tender tone.

"My cell phone. He must have taken it out of my purse and left this." She opened her hand.

Jim looked both ways up the road, frowning. He took the note that had so terrified her, handling it carefully by the edge. His easy mood vanished as he directed the penlight onto the paper. "Can you sit here by yourself?"

Crystal nodded, aware of his every move. There was something odd about his command of events, but she couldn't quite grasp what.

"I'll be right back," he promised, stroking a comforting hand over her hair.

Before she could wonder about his authoritative bearing, his touch had her mind veering away from anything analytical. Awareness of him as a powerful but gentle male flooded her. Why him? she wondered as she watched him walk to the front of the vehicle and tilt the page toward the headlights.

He looked like a big tawny cat the way he moved. He had a sort of jungle grace that made him seem almost dangerous. A deepening frown creased his forehead as he put the note on the hood and anchored it with the penlight.

"You guys have 911 up and running around here?" he asked, his voice gruff and almost businesslike.

"Yeah. It works for cell phones, too," she told him, wondering what on earth was wrong with her. She refused to use the excuse of a knock on the head and a near-fatal crash. She forced herself to think about that authority in his tone and her mind kicked in once again. What was it that seemed out of place about him? she asked herself.

As Crystal sat quietly trying to decide what bothered her about the way Jim was handling the situation, he pulled his cell phone out of his shirt pocket and punched in what she assumed was the emergency number. The murmur of his conversation with the dispatcher floated back to her, lulling her into closing her eyes. She couldn't seem to concentrate on analysis with his deep voice in the background. It was soothing. Almost hypnotizing.

"We'll be here," he said, now standing next to her. She looked up just as he ended the call.

"Where's your purse?" he asked.

She looked around. "I must have lost it. I had it at the car. I don't even remember dropping it."

"You were pretty scared."

"What do you want with my purse?"

"Whoever did this may not have worn gloves. I want to find it, but I don't want to leave you here in case he comes back. You think you're up to going back to your pickup?"

She felt less shaky and her headache was calming down a little, too. "I think so."

He smiled. "Good girl."

She went to push to her feet.

"No. Wait here for now. Just let me get a few things from the back. Then I'll have a look around on the road first," he said and went to the back of the SUV and opened the hatch. He returned with a large lantern-type flashlight and a box of plastic bags.

He shone the light on the road and found the skid marks leading off toward her truck and the scar her tires had left on the terrain. Next, he crouched down and looked at something. Crystal's curiosity got the better of her.

She stood carefully. Pleased that she was steadier on her feet, she walked to where he knelt. Using the plastic bag like a glove, he carefully picked up a piece of shiny trim that lay broken on the ground. After examining it, he turned the bag inside out around the trim then tied the bag shut. Why was he doing this?

"Uh…isn't that Sheriff King's job? Or at least Caleb's?" she asked, perplexed.

"There's a brushfire on the far side of town. The dispatcher, Mabel, I think she said, told me the two of them are tied up there helping until the smoke jumpers arrive."

"Mirabel. Don't ever call her Mabel or she'll hand you your head."

"Thanks for the warning," he said almost absently as he scanned the road with the big flashlight. But Crystal could see he was anything but absentminded. The movement of the light was careful and methodical. He was keenly attuned to his surroundings and more alive than she'd seen him before.

"Sheriff King's just as touchy about having his toes stepped on as Mirabel is about her name," she warned.

"I figured. When the dispatcher said he might be hours before getting here, I told her I'd secure the scene." He grinned. "Wouldn't want to make it an empty threat."

"Oh. I get it. He'll be here soon if only to stop you. How'd you know that would work?" she asked as he zeroed in on another shiny piece of chrome.

"Locals hate someone invading their territory. It's typical. King, well, I got the idea he was more than typical."

"You're very good at this. You must do extensive research."

"Research? No. No, it's experience." He picked up and bagged the newest piece of trim and stood, handing her a small wallet and shining the light on it.

She read it. Amazed. This explained a lot. And she'd been afraid of him? "You're a Pennsylvania state policeman? Lieutenant James R. Lovell," she read. "Ever get JR for a handle?"

He grinned. "Only from my mother. Anyone else gets their head handed to them."

"Thanks for the warning," she said, parroting his earlier words.

"You're sounding better. Ready to go hunting for clues?"

"Sure," she said, following him to the edge of the road. "So you're taking time off from work to try a new lifestyle or did you quit outright?" she asked, accepting his hand as she followed him into the shallow ditch. She had to fight to keep his touch from distracting her.

"I took leave. I wanted time to figure some things out. Thought I'd try to see if I could solve a mystery that wasn't job related."

"The…uh…the stalker book. Right?"

Jim swung around, directing the light toward the ground. He was still caught in the beams of his headlights because of the way he'd nosed the SUV inward toward the crash sight when he'd pulled to a stop. He looked momentarily disconcerted. "The stalker—

That's why you bolted yesterday. And tonight. You thought it was me. No wonder you ran.''

"I'm sorry. I—''

He held up his hand. "Don't apologize. Always go with a gut feeling. It can save your life. How long have the threats been going on?''

She tilted her head, staring at him. Once again she had to quickly reassess him. He hadn't been insulted by her distrust. "A few weeks. I never got a written one before. Just calls. I thought it was a high school kid's prank. My father and the sheriff thought so, too. I guess we were wrong.''

Jim was more than amazed. He was appalled. What kind of father would toss off a threat to his daughter? Jim didn't care if the woman in question had a black belt. No one had grieved more deeply or blamed himself more than Jessie's father when she'd been killed. Not even Jim. Alfonso Cushing's guilt over encouraging Jessie to take that last dangerous assignment had ultimately killed the thirty-five-year veteran of the force. Maybe Crystal's father hid his worry the way Alfonso Cushing had hidden his grief at the funeral. Grieving in private, dying in private by his own hand.

And Sheriff King should just plain be kicked out of office!

"A threat should never be taken lightly. I can't even wrap my mind around a police officer ignoring repeated threats. I'm appalled by the sheriff, but maybe your father just doesn't show his worry to you,'' he said, steadying her while she scaled the other side of the ditch. She was incredibly lucky her pickup hadn't rolled. He glanced ahead at the truck's trajectory and realized it was closer to a miracle. God and his angels had to have been watching over her because seat belt or no, she could have easily been killed in a roll. And the car that had hit her hadn't kept going, either. It had stopped, turned around and headed back toward town, he imagined by one of the roads that branched off this one.

"My father doesn't think twice about anything that won't benefit or harm the Circle A. If he's worried at all, it's over possibly losing a hand on the place. The date on that rental notice you answered was only a few days after Jackson lit out of here. Can't you tell he's real worried about what my brother's going through?" she said, her voice thick with sarcasm.

"Janie West said your father was angry at Jackson for leaving. Men sometimes do and say stupid things in anger."

"But that cabin had stood empty for years before my brother and I cleared it out and fixed it up for him to take over."

"Oh." Jim honestly didn't know what to say to that. He didn't know the man, after all, so he forced his mind back on to the problem at hand. Her missing purse. He couldn't bring himself to pump her for information on Jackson Alton and his abrupt departure anyway. Not when Jim had her blood on his hands and could see it still staining the side of her face and her shirt. Not when he couldn't forget how sad and alone she sounded or how frightened she'd been. And certainly not with the wreck of her pickup leaning crookedly against the tree.

Besides, he had other pressing questions that

needed answers. He swept the ground with the beam, looking for the purse, and found it on the ground next to the open door of the truck. After he bagged it and put it on the front seat, Jim looked back at Crystal. She stood still as a statue, staring at the taillights, her arms hugging her middle. She clearly hadn't forgotten the seriousness of the night's events for a second.

Jim walked back and dropped the gate, flipping the flashlight to its much-less-vibrant top-lantern mode. He then set it in the middle of the rear deck.

"Come on and sit before you fall," he told her. "If King or his deputy don't get here soon, we'll go on to the hospital."

"I don't need a hospital. I've been falling off horses my whole life. I've got a hard head. I'll be fine."

She sounded exhausted. Jim shook his head. "You said you'd blacked out. And you were a little confused there for a few minutes. You really need to be checked out."

"We'll see," she said, and sighed. "So how come you did the collecting evidence stuff to tweak Sheriff King?"

"A couple reasons. The dispatcher called him, and he refused to come out here even though I said this wasn't an accident. I don't trust that kind of stupidity, so I wanted to make sure he did this right. And because he should have taken my word that this was serious. He knows I'm a state police detective back home."

She frowned. "How would he know that?"

Jim had never intended to hide his profession. His

cover story was all the more believable because of it and he didn't have to lie this way. Also, he'd decided that if the sheriff found out Jim was there to check into Jackson Alton's background, he'd be bound by ethics to secrecy.

"I checked in with him before heading out to the Circle A yesterday. Since I have my weapon with me it's more than likely a legality. But I also felt it was an ethical and a professional courtesy."

Crystal curved her spine and rolled gracefully back to lay on the rear deck of the pickup with her legs bent at the knee and her heels on the edge of the gate. She laced her fingers behind her head and smiled up at him. "Ah. There was your mistake. He wouldn't understand that."

Jim chuckled, glad she was calming down a little more and that her keen sense of humor was returning. So he could turn and look at her without craning his neck, he hoisted his leg onto the lift gate further and turned his body toward her.

And his heart skipped.

In the low light created by the lantern and the moonlight, Jim found himself gazing down at the most exotic, natural beauty he'd ever seen. He swallowed with some difficulty.

"Which part wouldn't he understand?" he asked, his voice sounding strained even to himself.

"All three. *Professional* and *ethical* are words in a dictionary he may never have heard. Joe King was a bully from elementary school days. Between his father's money and his star athlete status, he's never had to learn a real work ethic. I also don't think he has more than a nodding acquaintance with Colorado law. Luckily, other than an occasional barroom brawl or a kid shoplifting, he has very little crime to handle. In November it looks as if he'll be out of office, thus correcting a huge local mistake. As in, his election. So, tell me, what is Pennsylvania like?''

Jim looked up at the stars above that seemed so close he felt as if he could grab one. He glanced back at her and once again had a tough time swallowing. Right then, if he could, he'd hand her one of those stars just to see her smile again.

Confused, he'd come to Colorado to get away from the job. It was supposed to be an easy task to investigate a man he was nearly positive had no nefarious motives. The trip was mostly about time to reassess his life. And what happens? He meets a woman who can muddle his brain with one look and who complicated everything because of who she was.

Sometimes Jim wondered at God's sense of humor. He really did.

Chapter Five

"What's Pennsylvania like?" Jim repeated, trying to concentrate on the conversation and not the stars above, Crystal's smile or anything else with a romantic bent. He thought of the golden fields he'd found as he drove westward. The flat plains that seemed to go on forever. And the craggy mountains far in the distance.

"Green. It's really green. I didn't realize how green till I came here. Even inside Philadelphia there's a huge park called Fairmont Park. It used to be the largest metropolitan park in the world." He shrugged. "It still could be for all I know. It has its own police force."

"Then you haven't had the drought conditions we have."

"We've been in and out of a drought for several years now but it's still, well, green."

"I thought it was almost all concrete and asphalt."

Jim chuckled. "Right. And everyone back home

thinks Colorado is all mountainous, but we don't have any place as flat as these plains. I will say your mountains are impressive. Ours are much less dramatic. They're covered with trees. Which makes them—''

''Green,'' she put in with a chuckle of her own. ''I'd love to see it sometime. It must be wonderful being able to take time off the way you have to try something new and to see the country.''

Jim was about to comment that he hadn't really had a choice. Not if he wanted to make it to his next birthday without getting himself killed. In the distance he noticed the flashing light bars of a couple of police cruisers.

''Well, look who decided to join us. You rest. I'll meet this yahoo up on the road.''

''Bless you. The less I have to deal with Sheriff King, the better.''

Jim snickered and strolled off toward a meeting with Sheriff Joseph King and another taller man he assumed was the deputy Crystal had mentioned. Caleb. Both men were within five years of each other in age but only one looked fit, and it sure wasn't King. The sheriff of Torrence hadn't impressed Jim at all when they'd met.

''Well, look here, Caleb. He's the smart fella from the East. You wasted your time out here securing the *crime* scene. I don't believe for one minute that Cris Alton got run off the road by some phantom car. She's been tearing up and down this road since she turned sixteen. Looks like she couldn't make the curve and she's looking for excuses for wrecking part of her daddy's work fleet.''

Jim easily held on to his temper. It wasn't the first

time he'd run up against blatant incompetence. His task was made all the easier when the other man stepped forward and extended his hand. "Hi, there. I'm Deputy Caleb Hart. Would you mind telling us why you think this is a crime scene?"

Smart, Jim thought. Got his question asked without insulting his boss.

"Well, there's the fact that Crystal says a car hit hers and I can't see a single reason to doubt her word. Then there's the light-colored paint embedded in the brand-new dent on the driver's side of the pickup, which to me pretty much proves she was hit."

"That's enough for me," Caleb said.

"There's more. She's already complained about threatening phone calls to your office."

Caleb Hart frowned at his boss. "You didn't say anything to me about phone calls, Joe."

Sheriff King hiked his pants up to his waist again and squared his shoulders. "Don't see what that has to do with this. That was just a bunch of high school boys feeling their oats."

Jim went on as if the sheriff hadn't spoken. He pointed to the note on the SUV's hood, still anchored with his penlight. "There's also the threatening note she found in her purse where her cell phone should have been. At best, someone wanted her out here alone and terrified. At worst, he wanted her dead. It's a miracle she didn't roll coming up on the other side of the ditch, especially since she was unconscious by then."

Jim gestured to the note again. "I'm afraid Crystal had the note pretty balled up in her hand by the time I got here. I bagged her purse, in case the stalker left prints when he switched the cell phone for the note. It's on the front seat of the pickup.''

"What'd you do with Cris? Or did one of the Circle A's men come get her?'' the sheriff asked.

"She's resting in the back of the truck. She was pretty badly shaken and banged up. It would help if you could help convince her to go to the hospital to be looked at,'' he told Caleb Hart.

Caleb shook his head. "She busted a collarbone in the Fourth of July rodeo a few years back. Not only wouldn't she go to the hospital, but she rode in a second event. I don't know as I've ever met a more stubborn female.''

"That's no female, Caleb,'' Sheriff King sneered. "That's an Amazon. Ain't natural for a woman to look a man in the eye the way she can. Which is why this stalker theory is all wrong. No man would spare her a second look.''

So that was the problem. Sheriff King wasn't just stupid. He was blind, as well. The sound of Crystal's approach kept Jim from putting forward that undiplomatic theory.

"Well, it's clear one man in the area isn't blind,'' he just couldn't help saying. "Trouble is this one's also dangerous,'' Jim added and turned away to help Crystal climb the ditch wall.

"Sheriff. Deputy,'' she said to both men in a mocking tone.

"Exciting night, eh, Cris?'' Caleb said, clearly taking in the blood on her chambray shirt as he reached out to shake her hand. He'd also spoken with quite a bit of irony in his voice.

"Excitement I could have done without," she said, taking his proffered hand.

"So you say someone ran you off the road," Sheriff King said.

"No. Someone *did* run me off the road. Huge difference. He came out of nowhere and sideswiped me. The car was silver or white."

Hart, who'd already flipped open a notebook scribbled something down and asked, "Make? Model?"

"Sorry. It was just a flash out of the corner of my eye as the car hit me. I cracked my head on the side window a second later. Before I knew it, I was coming to and my truck had gotten too friendly with that tree," she said, pointing to the crash site.

"The car that hit her stopped, turned around and spun rubber going in the other direction," Jim put in. "He didn't pass me so he must have turned off one of the side roads."

"It looks as if you were wrong with the high school prank theory, Sheriff," Crystal said. "A teenage boy would have to worry about his parents seeing a dent."

King gave off a long-suffering sigh. "Cris, you got to use your head. Who'd be stalking you? Anyone thinking on asking you out would just do it. I mean, it isn't like anyone else ever asks you."

Okay, Jim thought. Now that about tears it! Before he could put the unprofessional sheriff in his place, Crystal did it neatly.

Her lips just sort of eased into a smirk and she crossed her arms across her chest. "Except for you, Joe," she said lazily. "You've asked me several times, but I'm not that desperate yet and I doubt I ever will be." She turned her back on King. "Jim, could you give me a lift home?"

Caleb Hart snickered and followed her to the passenger door of Jim's SUV. He helped her in. "You go on over to the clinic and get checked out."

"I don't need anything but a nice hot bath and bed."

"Maybe not but I'll need something official for my report. You do want us to investigate. Right?"

"Of course. But what has that got to do with me going to see Doc Reynolds?"

"Because if he fills out an accident report, we'd have to investigate and King can't get around that. Rules are rules. I don't make them. No official injury. No investigation. It's part of King's budget-cutting measures."

She sighed. "Caleb, I'm telling you you'd better win that election in November. The man might have been a good quarterback, but as a sheriff, he's a twit!" She leaned back in her seat before turning her head toward him. "Jim, would you mind taking me back to town first?"

Jim was glad Hart closed her door because the darkness hid his grin. Yeah. Caleb Hart was quick on his feet, all right.

The next morning, Crystal woke feeling as if she'd been run over by a truck instead of having had her pickup run off the road. After she showered and gingerly washed her hair, she dressed then made her way to the kitchen for a cup of Anna's coffee.

Anna was married to Tomas, the Circle A's horse wrangler, and had been living on the ranch all of

Crystal's life. She used to help Crystal's grandmother with the heavy cleaning until she took over as housekeeper when the old woman died.

Crystal grimaced when she found her father still in the breakfast room reading a periodical over the remnants of breakfast.

"It's about time you decided to grace us with your presence," her father grumbled from behind his magazine. "Is this the kind of hours you keep when I'm away on trips?"

"No," she said, her teeth clenched. "I had a little trouble on the road last night. I'm afraid my pickup's a total wreck."

He looked up and scowled. "What happened?"

Anna bustled into the room then with a basket of laundry tucked under her arm. "There is blood all over the shirt you wore yesterday. What happened?"

"I had an accident with my pickup," she said, and patted the older woman on her plump shoulder. "It was just a little cut on the head. You know how head wounds bleed. I'm afraid those phone calls I've been getting are more than just annoying."

Crystal glanced at her father, trying to gauge his reaction to both her injury and his misjudgment of the danger. "Apparently, the guy's threats were serious. He ran me off the road."

"Oh! You must have been terrified!" Anna exclaimed.

Not wanting to upset her, Crystal shrugged, trying to look cool and calm when she was anything but. "Actually it happened so fast I hardly had time to react before I cracked my head. Doc Reynolds says I only have a slight concussion but—" she chuckled, again trying to lessen Anna's worry while letting her father know she wasn't up to too much physical work "—I feel like I bruised every bone in my body. Every muscle, too. I'm better than the truck, though. It looked terminal."

"What you need is a good breakfast. You sit down and tell us all about what happened."

"How do you know it was the guy who's been calling you?" her father asked.

"Because when I went into my purse for my cell phone it was gone and had been replaced with a threatening note."

"At least you saw Doc Reynolds," Anna said, a grateful sigh in her voice as she set a heavenly smelling cup of coffee on the table in front of Crystal.

"Oh, bless you," she sighed, and looked up into Anna's sweet warm face. "Stop looking so worried. Doc gave me a clean bill of health."

"I don't call a concussion a clean bill of health," her father said, but rather than sounding concerned, he seemed annoyed. "When did he say you can ride again? I've decided to pull the herds in closer to well water. Half-pint Spring isn't the only water hole going dry."

Two whole minutes focused on me and not his precious ranch. This might be some kind of record. So much for telling him how bad I feel.

The thought of climbing into the saddle and driving a bunch of cantankerous cattle didn't appeal to Crystal on the best of days. And this wasn't the best of days. It wouldn't do any good to voice her complaint, however, because he wouldn't hear her anyway. "First I have to call this into the insurance company and notify my cell phone provider. After that I guess I can ride today.''

"Where's the pickup?'' her father asked, dragging her out of depressing thoughts.

She grimaced. "Out on 17 kissing a tree. I'll handle having it towed into Vern's station. The adjuster can look at it there.''

"And you should call Doc Reynolds,'' Anna ordered. "I know you would never think to ask if it's safe to ride, and you should. A concussion is nothing to play with. Your grandmother would never forgive me if I didn't make you check.''

Evan Alton shot his housekeeper an annoyed look and sat a bit straighter. "If the pickup is out of commission, and your cell phone was stolen, how did you get home last night?''

"Actually, Jim Lovell found me a while after I came to.'' She went on to describe the night, its revelations and all its implications.

"So that big blond hunk is a policeman,'' Anna said. "Good. He can protect you.''

It was on the tip of Crystal's tongue to say she didn't need protection, but then she remembered how frightened she'd been and how safe she'd felt in Jim's embrace. Remembering his tender ministrations and concern had warmth spreading through her once again. Jim was so different from the men in her experience.

She remembered the greatly stifled Joseph King of last night and grinned. "I don't know what Jim Lovell said before I got to the road, but I never saw Joe King do less swaggering than he did last night. Jim was appalled by our sheriff, by the way, so he played with him by securing the crime scene, Pennsylvania State Police-style.''

''And Lovell thinks this guy is dangerous?'' her father asked.

''Yes, he does, Dad.''

Evan Alton's scowl deepened. ''Then maybe it would be smart for you to stay put on the Circle A until the sheriff's office can find this person.''

That would suit her father just fine. Then she could spend every waking hour except Sunday morning and Wednesday night working to maintain or expand his precious Circle A.

Before she could come up with an appropriate comment, Anna spoke up. ''Or perhaps Mr. Lovell would go with you when you do feel the need to leave the Circle A,'' Anna suggested.

Her father grunted, his nose back in *The Cattleman's Journal*. Crystal picked at her meal, feeling pushed aside and like a part of the equipment around the Circle A. Even Anna, a hired housekeeper, cared more about the implications and danger of this stalker than her father did.

Chapter Six

Later that morning, at around ten, Crystal saw Jim talking to Caleb Hart when she was on her way to the barn, so she changed directions and walked toward them. If the sheriff's office had learned something, she wanted to know. Engrossed in conversation, the men sat on the little stone porch of Jackson's cabin, but both stood when she approached. She wasn't used to such courtesies. Deputy Hart, she thought sardonically, had followed Jim Lovell's example, arriving on his feet a second or two behind the Circle A's newest resident.

"Cris, I saw Vern towing your pickup as I left town," Caleb said.

"I have to meet my insurance adjuster there at twelve. I'm afraid it's a waste of time, but I'd like to try talking him into saving it if I can. Did your office find any light-colored cars with damage?"

"Afraid there's nothing yet."

"How about anything on the paint and the chrome pieces?"

"I sent samples of the paint and the pieces of trim to the state lab, but it'll take time. I was just telling Jim here that they're pretty backed up. Murder cases get priority. I suggested to the sheriff that he call back and explain that we're trying to keep you alive and that we don't want priority assigned to the case later because it's become a murder case."

Crystal felt the blood drain from her head as Jim growled, "Deputy," and sent a quelling glare at Caleb.

She'd heard the caller's voice and had read the note, but the threat became more real when Caleb acknowledged its deadliness. "You think he really means to kill me. Not just scare me. Right?"

"I'm sorry, Cris. Sometimes I'm so used to you being one of the guys, I forget you're a woman. Jim's promised to look out for you and I'll try stepping up my patrols out this way."

Crystal shifted her eyes toward Jim. She stared, her heart thundering. Suddenly Jim Lovell was all she could think about. He'd almost kissed her beneath the streetlight last night. For the first time in her memory she'd felt feminine and desirable. Then later, after he'd found her, cared for her, she'd known what it felt like to be protected. And she'd liked it. And now...

"You promised to look out for me?" she asked, feeling curiously breathless.

"Your father asked me to keep an eye on you. He's very worried."

Now there was a letdown. And an impossible claim, too. "*My* father?"

"Give the guy a break," Caleb Hart snapped. "You and Jackson act as if your dad's an ogre. You two should have had my father."

Crystal silently acknowledged Caleb's perspective. Caleb's father was a monster.

"We do *not* act as if Dad is anything but what he is. A man totally centered on this ranch and his grief over my mother's death, to the exclusion of all else, his children included. A man can be a workaholic and not work in Denver. We know he's a good man and that we could have done worse. But we also know *he* could have done better. Sheriff Barrett did better by you and you weren't even his son."

Caleb gave her a slightly sheepish nod that said, "Granted."

"So *did* the sheriff call the state lab?" she asked.

"Not till your father raised the roof right before I came out here."

Crystal pondered this and turned toward Jim again without further comment. A frown creased the tall blonde's forehead. "Didn't you say Joe King had asked you out several times?"

"And I turned him down just as often. Why?"

"Generally, men in small towns don't ask a woman out if they don't have at least some feelings for her already. So why is he so insistent on not protecting her?" he asked, directing his question to Caleb. It was a query from one professional to another. The words of the note, burned in her brain since reading them, thundered through her thoughts. *Remember, I'm watching you. I can have you with me whenever I choose. Reject me again and you'll die.*

Caleb's voice brought her back to the present. "I'd say he's holding a grudge. He's never been one to lose gracefully. Are you thinking *he* could be the stalker? I wasn't with him all the time last night at that brushfire, but I don't see how he could get from one side of town to the other that fast. Then again, the fire was arson. I guess he could have done it but… I don't think much of him as a sheriff or a man, but I can't see him doing this. I just can't."

"Neither can I, really. So far, this guy's been pretty smart. Joe King isn't as dumb as he looks, but I doubt he's this smart, either."

"So, have you made this a working vacation or are you steeping yourself in this to use in your book? Sort of killing two birds with one stone?" Caleb asked.

Jim shrugged carelessly, but there was something odd in his eyes. "They say truth is stranger than fiction. And atmosphere in a book lends to its believability."

"You'll get plenty of ranching atmosphere in the next two weeks. Dad wants to round up and drive the herds in close. Several of our outlying water holes have dried up. We need to get the cattle to a reliable water source so we don't lose them to thirst or to mud the way we almost lost that calf Wednesday."

"Hold on. I promised I'd ride into Torrence with you when you go in. But I can't exactly follow you around on the ranch except here at the homestead."

Was that reticence in his voice? If so, it made no sense. Why was following her around a problem when it would give him the chance to do firsthand research for his book? "What happened to soaking up the atmosphere and using it?"

"I'll use it and I'm glad to pitch in to keep you safe. As long as I can do it from the front seat of my vehicle or on foot, that is."

"For the next two weeks that won't put you in my proximity, then. The day after tomorrow I'll be allowed to ride with the men again."

"You'll be a perfect target in the midst of the confusion and isolation of a roundup," Caleb said, frowning. "You really ought to not be riding off alone after strays for instance."

"Would Sheriff King appoint someone to ride with her?" Jim Lovell asked.

"That'd be me, and no, he won't go that far to appease her father. There's no way he'll pull me off patrol to watch one person. A person he seems to think is trying to get her daddy's attention with this stalker talk."

"Oh, for crying out loud! As if I'd pull a juvenile stunt like that! And how does he account for the paint on my pickup?"

Caleb shrugged. "I didn't say there was any logic to his claim, and you have to admit your dad approaching Jim to watch you and raising the roof with King earlier adds weight to his theory. And that said, I still don't think riding out without Jim in tow is a good idea."

Jim wasted no time disabusing Caleb of his assumption. "I don't ride. There was very little call for that growing up in Riverside."

Now wasn't this interesting? He didn't sound inexperienced. He sounded afraid, she decided and couldn't help but smirk. "I do believe our volunteer cop is afraid of riding, Caleb."

Jim wasn't about to deny his feelings. He was too old to put up a front to impress anyone—man or woman. They could think he was so chicken, he clucked! He really didn't care.

"I'm not afraid of riding. In a car. In an airplane. On a boat. On a bus, train or subway, either," he added for good measure, "but no way am I riding a horse. No way, no how. I'm here doing research and I'm not going home in traction or a box."

Caleb Hart chuckled, then sobered. "Then I strongly suggest you stay put around here, Cris. I don't want to scare you again, but this guy could be one of your men. As I said, it can get pretty isolated out there. Think about it. Both of you." He looked at his pocket watch. "I'll leave you two to work out a compromise while I get back on patrol."

Crystal stared after Caleb Hart. Her annoyance was easy to read, but the deputy was right. It could be one of their men.

"So what's a good cop like Hart doing playing second banana to a nitwit like King?"

"Poor Caleb. He was the town's bad boy when we were kids until Sheriff Barrett reined him in." She grimaced. "So when Joe King, star high school quarterback, ran against Caleb in a special election to replace Barrett for the rest of his term, Joe won. Even with Sheriff Barrett's support, Caleb lost badly. He stayed on as deputy, though. He joked to me that someone has to protect the town from Joe's incompetence, but I think he really needs to prove himself here, where his family name is synonymous with trash. Hopefully, this year will prove Joe King's undoing and Caleb will win the town's confidence in time.''

"You mentioned the election last night. If he wins you'll have another—what—four years of that yahoo?''

''I'm not really all that worried. His popularity's begun slipping. He's just not competent. He cuts corners the way he always has but it matters now. And he can't seem to help himself from playing favorites.''

"And you aren't one of his favorites.''

"None of the Altons ever were since Jackson beat the daylights out of him when we were kids. He'd been teasing me about being part Cheyenne, and Jackson put a stop to it even though my brother was three years younger than Joey.''

Jim did the math and silently cheered the absent Jackson for defending his younger sister against the bully. "Still, this is a long time to carry a grudge,'' he said.

''Except that Joe cried in front of all his classmates. Dad tried to make Jackson apologize, but he wouldn't give him the satisfaction. Then, years later, Jackson replaced him as quarterback after Joe graduated high school. My brother broke every school record King had set.''

"I'll bet your brother wasn't too happy to have him be elected sheriff.''

"The special election came up after my brother—left. He hasn't called home, so Jackson doesn't know." She paused with a frown furrowing a crease between her eyebrows. "Tell me why you don't want to learn to ride. You almost sounded afraid."

Jim recognized a change of subject when he heard one but, once again, couldn't bring himself to push her about her brother. Not when merely mentioning his name put such a heart-rending mixture of frustration and sadness in her voice. She clearly felt the absence of her brother keenly.

"That was exactly what you heard," he readily admitted. "How anyone can climb on the back of a thousand pounds of uncontrollable animal is beyond me. It made me nervous just watching you ride Wednesday."

"Your first mistake is believing they're uncontrollable."

Jim thought of Cole Taggert back at Laurel Glen Horse Farm, the man on whose behalf he was in Colorado. Cole Taggert's mother was killed before his eyes by a crazed horse and his anger had nearly destroyed his relationship with his father, Ross. No, he wasn't buying her claim, but he could hardly use the Taggerts' loss as an example.

"No way," he declared instead. "I've watched rodeos and those bucking broncos and the riders who climb aboard them. They're out of their gourds!"

Crystal laughed. "Those men know exactly what they're doing, and the horses are bred to buck that way. We buy horses bred to listen to their riders and we train them to listen. When I ride Lady, I do it with complete confidence that she knows what she's doing and does as I say because I'm boss. She loves me. And I love her."

He eyed her incredulously. "You *love* your horse."

"Don't be that way. Didn't you ever have a pet?"

"I did," he responded seriously. "And he slept with me every night. I assume you don't let Lady sleep with you. I only mention this because if Ralph rolled over, I didn't die of a crushed chest cavity."

Crystal laughed and he found he'd been craving the sound since the last time he'd heard it.

"You really have to give it a try. I can tell you, whenever I read a book with horses in it, if the author hasn't got experience with them it shows. The facts sound like research, not tone and mood and ambience." She looked at her watch. "Maybe when I get back from Vern's you'll want to at least walk down to the barn with me. Lady has a friend she works with named Duke. I think you'd learn a lot from him if you gave him half a chance."

"Sure, but you mean when *we* get back from Vern's, right?"

She shot him an electric grin he felt down to his toes. "It's been a long time since I had a baby-sitter, but I have to admit I appreciate it."

Jim stood. "So let's get going." He frowned, remembering what was odd about her invitation to the barn. "I thought the guy who takes care of the livestock was Tomas?"

"It is. Duke's a big quarter horse." She laughed again, but this time the joke was on him.

Chapter Seven

The ride to and from town was uneventful. By the time he and Crystal got to Vern's Garage and Body Shop, her pickup had been declared dead. All that was left for her to do was to clear it out and prepare it for a decent burial in Vern's auto dump and used-parts lot. Jim looked at it himself and concurred. There was no fixing the pickup.

"You really have a car that old?" she asked him, breaking the comfortable silence that had fallen between them on the way home.

"Ruby isn't just old. She's a classic! A candy-apple-red, 1965 Mustang will never be just plain old."

"And that's how you learned so much about cars?"

Jim glanced over at her and smiled at the memory. "I restored it with a couple of friends and our fathers. It's too complex a piece of machinery to chance driving it cross-country so I rented this," he finished, absently missing Ruby and all the car represented to him.

He'd looked over the five acres of dream cars, feeling a poignant blast from the past.

It had been a day much like this when they'd all picked out the most likely restoration candidate—a tired-looking, primer—gray Mustang with a few minor dents, no chrome and lots of "possibilities."

And it had been a day much like this when Tommy Peterson died of a drug overdose, sending Jim and Tommy's brother, Greg, into police work. While Tom would remain a teenager forever in his thoughts, Greg had grown into an admirable man who had eventually come to the conclusion that being a cop wasn't God's plan for him. He'd gone into the ministry, having found his true path. Jim now had to wonder if, in his grief and anger, he, too, had misinterpreted God's plan.

"...envy you," he finally heard Crystal saying.

Embarrassed for missing all but tail end of her thought, Jim frowned. "I'm sorry?"

"I said I envy you. It must have been nice to be that close to your father."

"Dad was first-rate. He was a decorated cop and a great man, but his kids were his greatest joy and accomplishment."

"Was? Is he gone?"

As he steered the SUV around a tight bend, then into the long Circle A drive, he fought off a wave of sadness. He guessed he'd always miss his dad. "Yeah. He was killed two years ago trying to negotiate a domestic situation. Greg's the only one left who worked on Ruby with me.''

"Greg. Your friend the pastor? The one who brought you to the Lord?''

Jim nodded, ridiculously flattered that she remembered something he'd said in passing. "One and the same. After Greg was shot in the line of duty for the second time in way less than a year, he got the message God had been sending him for years.''

Jim parked in the lot between the back of the main house and the cabin and walked around to get her door, but Crystal had already opened it and stepped to the ground. She blushed and grimaced when their gazes met. "Sorry, I'm not used to...''

"Men who aren't blind,'' he finished, annoyed for her and all women with a little stature to them. Joy, his beautiful sister, came to mind. As far as he knew, the only male in her life was the little twin-engine Cessna she called George after her godfather, an ex-cop who'd given her the chance to learn to soar through the clouds.

Crystal smiled shyly. "They aren't blind. I'm just paying the price for having been a tomboy with an older brother for a best friend. I was one of the guys before we all noticed there was a difference between them and me.'' She shrugged. "I guess it was too late for them to make the mental transition by then.''

Once again, there was that wistfulness in her tone when she spoke of her brother. This time, though, he knew he had to push. He was becoming too attuned to her and her moods and knew that when coupled with the attraction he felt for her, his peace of mind was in danger. What little peace of mind he still had!

He had to finish this and get out of town.

"I have the same sort of relationship with my sister."

"So she knows all about why you're here, then? What you're searching for?"

Jim was stunned. How did Crystal know he was searching for anything but a part-time job as a writer? Did she mean the soul-searching he'd planned to do on this trip west, or his hunt for her brother's motive for being at Laurel Glen?

"Searching for?" he asked.

She shot him a knowing grin. "You think you're getting the same message from God your friend Greg got. Isn't that what the book and the leave of absence are about?"

Though he wasn't comfortable having revealed either fact, he was so relieved she hadn't caught on to his investigation. He found it easier to talk about the inner turmoil than he would have thought possible. And truthfully, Crystal was easy to talk to. Easier even than Joy, and that was really saying something.

"I'm not sure yet," he admitted only a little reluctantly, "but I'm listening." Or trying to. *God just isn't talking loud enough.*

"Were you...you know...shot or something, like your friend and your father?"

"Almost. They say 'almost' only counts in horseshoes and hand grenades, but slugs from a Saturday-night special can be a pretty effective wake-up call even when they hit the wall just next to you."

"What drew you to police work?"

"I wanted to make a difference. Maybe be like my dad, but truthfully, it was losing Greg's brother to drugs that pushed me over the edge and into it as a career. Greg, too, but it turned out he was trying to work through guilt for missing the signs of drug use in Tom."

"Then you think your father had it wrong?"

Jim stared at her, trying to follow her logic and realized it was actually his logic she'd followed, and the answer came out all wrong. "No. Dad was born to be a cop. He died doing what he loved. Saving lives. Helping people."

"Then why is a near-miss telling you police work isn't for you?"

Jim didn't know and told her so. "So how come you stayed here to work on a ranch?" he asked after vowing to think long and hard about what Crystal had said.

She shrugged. "I guess I was born into my career, even though there are aspects of it right now that I dislike. There are others I couldn't imagine not having in my life."

"What are the parts you dislike?"

"The foreman job. It's my brother's. I don't want it. He did, but my father wouldn't let him do it."

"Does he let you?"

She shook her head. "His interference doesn't bother me, though, because it isn't my job. I want to go back to just handling the business aspects of the ranch."

"So you're the financial whiz and your brother and father run the place."

She let out a wistful sigh. "Except that Jackson thinks we should move into horse breeding and Dad wants to stick strictly to cattle. All they did was argue about how best to handle the Circle A's future."

"Is that why your brother left?"

"He had lots of reasons, but Dad was the center of all of them."

A whinny drew Crystal's attention, and she turned away, but not before Jim saw the pain in her eyes. He felt like a first-class heel and knew he couldn't keep probing the wound. He'd have to get his information another way.

"Lady's putting on a quite a show," Crystal said, and chuckled, the low timbre playing over his nerve endings like a warm breath.

Jim followed her gaze and grinned in spite of a growing sense of doom those two horses in the corral created in him. "The horses are the part of the ranch you don't think you could live without, I assume."

She nodded and smiled. "Come on. You promised to give Duke a chance to win you over."

"Let's qualify that. You tricked me into it."

"You still agreed. See that big black off to Lady's left, the one who looks bored? That's Duke."

"You really think that enormous horse looks bored? Maybe he just can't move his big feet."

Crystal laughed. "Oh, he's much too hard a worker to be happy being left to loll around all day. He's my brother's horse. And he's Lady's brother. He's so well trained he's nearly intuitive. And he isn't enormous. Nor are his feet all that big. Now a Clydes-dale's an enormous horse—their feet, too. At seven-teen and a half hands, Duke's big for a quarter horse, but not as big as one of those big old draft horses.''

As they walked closer, Jim thought of Jackson Al-ton's advice the day they'd met at Laurel Glen. Cole Taggert had been looking for an excuse to introduce the two of them, thinking Jim would understand his worry over the new foreman after meeting him.

The surprise of the resemblance between the men of the Taggert family and Jack Alton had been over-shadowed by Jim's shock on hearing Cole tell Alton that Jim was there to learn to ride. Crystal's brother had taken one look at Jim and had seen his fear. He'd suggested Jim learn to work with horses in the stable before considering riding. He'd told him it was dan-gerous to ride scared.

Jim stopped in his tracks when Lady reared up on her back legs and trumpeted. Oh, he was scared, all right! ''I'm not doing this.''

''She's showing off for you,'' Crystal cajoled.

''Then she can do it from there, and I'm staying put right here.''

Crystal rolled her eyes and turned away. She walked to the corral and opened the gate, letting out a shrill whistle. Both horses moved her way, and Jim himself was nearly mesmerized. Their muscles rip-pled under coats that shone like satin in the sunlight. They were really beautiful animals. There was no de-nying it. But he was sure he'd rather admire them from afar.

Speaking to them in low, nearly hypnotic tones, Crystal drew Jim closer almost against his will.

"Isn't your sister just the biggest show-off west of the Mississippi?" she said, accepting a butt on the shoulder from Duke as she stroked Lady's muzzle. "See that big guy over there? I'd bet a month's worth of apples he'd wind up riding you if you were real sweet to him." The horse snuffled and shook his head. "Well, yeah, he is a little worried about riding, but if anyone can overcome that, you can. Go on. Go make up to him. No one should miss all the fun we have 'cause they're afraid to ride. Wouldn't that be a sad thing to send him off back home to the big city without him feeling the wind in his face as you fly across the plains?"

"Wouldn't it be sadder to send him home in traction on one of his sister's Angel Flights?" Jim said from right behind her.

Crystal jumped, her heart pounding in her chest. How had he gotten so close without her noticing and without either of the horses reacting to his movement? The answer was easy.

The man moved like a cat. Nothing hurried or jerky, even when he was terrified.

Just silent. Stealthy.

She'd noticed it before and was more sure than ever that he was doing exactly the job God had prepared him for. Writing was nice for a hobby but someone like Jim would never be happy with fiction. Not when he could live the real thing.

Crystal, taking a cue from Duke, turned toward Jim. "There are a lot of things to know about horses, but the most important is not to approach a horse from the back or directly in front because they have a limited field of vision. It's best to approach from the shoulder or as near the neck as possible. You just did that quite by accident. It's a good idea to speak softly and call his name as you approach because he may be asleep. Extend your hand and pat him on the neck or shoulder once you get up to him. Later I'll show you how to approach him in a stall.''

Jim did as she told him. "He's very soft."

Crystal shot him a wise smirk. "Oohhh... You were afraid of a giant stuffed animal?''

"Fear can be a healthy thing," he said as he smoothed his hand over Duke's smooth jaw. But the animal's soft eyes called to him. Surely it would show there if he were really dangerous. And since when did Jim shy away from danger anyway?

He couldn't believe he was saying this. "You know, I think I *would* like to try riding.''

Chapter Eight

❧

Crystal eyed Jim, trying to decide if his abrupt turn-around about riding was really more about increased confidence than false bravado. For years she'd stood on the sidelines at rodeos, watching otherwise intelligent men make near martyrs of themselves while foolishly trying to impress the women.

Women other than herself, of course.

She nearly grinned as a thought occurred to her. Was Jim trying to impress *her?* Now wouldn't that be something! But no, Crystal lectured herself, she didn't want Jim trying to impress her by getting into a macho contest of wills with Jackson's animal. Instead, she wanted him to share her love of riding.

"You're sure? I don't want you up on Duke if you're still terrified. A horse needs to be confident of his rider. He'd feel your fear and that would make him skittish. It could get dangerous."

"Don't worry. I'm not afraid anymore. Really. It's strange. Now that I'm close up to them, they aren't as intimidating as they were from far away and, I guess, as they were in my imagination.''

''You heard a scary story, right? About a crazed stallion killing someone?''

Jim blinked and lost a little color. ''Uh...I... well...yeah.''

Crystal's heart fell. She'd made him nervous again. Why had she brought up horses that have killed people? she chided herself.

Before she could even try to reassure him, though, he went on to explain, ''When I was a rookie cop in Riverside, a state cop visited our precinct. It was the day after a woman out his way was killed by a horse. It was in all the papers and on the news. One of the veteran cops, who used to work as a mounted policeman in Philly, asked what had happened. It turned out the statie had responded to the call. I guess the imagery of what he described sort of stuck. I've never forgotten her name or the name of the farm,'' he added after a pause.

''Jim, an incident like that is rarer than lightning hitting someone.''

''Then I guess you heard about it?''

''I doubt it. I'm guessing I'd have been a teenager at the time. Between school and chores on the ranch, I barely had time to sleep in those days.'' She chuckled sardonically. ''Not that much has changed in that area since then. The horse world is small but Pennsylvania is pretty far away.''

So very far away, she thought wistfully. Far away and now not only would it have Jackson, but when Jim left it would have him, as well.

With some effort she shook off that unsettling thought and added a lead rope to Lady and Duke's halters. She showed Jim how to lead the horse, and they walked the animals into the stable. After she put Lady in her stall, Crystal showed Jim where the tack was kept.

Working with Duke magically seemed to settle Jim's nerves again, so she showed him how to bridle, saddle, and check to make sure the saddle was tight. Mounting came next, which would, of course, be followed by dismounting.

The only problem was that the mounting didn't go quite as smoothly as Crystal planned. As instructed, Jim stood in the now-empty corral facing the back of the horse. He placed his left hand—the one holding the reins—on Duke's neck in front of his withers, and put his left foot in the stirrup just as she'd shown him to do. But when he grasped the pummel with his right hand to bounce and swing into the saddle, Duke side-stepped and moved forward, dragging Jim backward and off the foot that still remained on terra firma.

Jim promptly landed in a heap in the dusty corral. A chorus of hoots floated on the breeze from a group of Circle A cowhands.

"What happened?" Jim asked, looking up at her, clearly stunned.

"Duke just initiated you. He was being so good, I forgot to warn you. I am so sorry." She rushed to help him up while throwing a black look at the men. "He's done that to every man who's tried to ride him since Jackson left," she said pointedly and loud enough to be heard clear over to where the hyenas were whooping it up.

"Then I'll just have to give it another try," he said, his jaw squared with determination.

The whole process repeated itself twice more. Jim's jeans now wore more dirt than the corral floor, and the hands were having a high-old time at his expense.

"Okay, that's it. I'll hold him," she said, jumping back down off the fence. She was not about to let Jim continue as the butt of the men's jokes. They were a good group, but there was something about weakness in another man that brought out the high school prankster in all of the cowhands. Between the six of them, she doubted their mental age equaled half Jim's.

Jim glanced back at the men, then at her shaking her head. "No. You said I have to show him who's boss. If I'm going to ride with you in two days, he and I need to come to an understanding, now. I figure he's just like a dog." He traced Duke from hoof to head then tail. "Granted, a big dog, but he's an animal. Right?"

She nodded.

"Then if I let you help, he'll think he's beaten me. I doubt you helped anyone else he's dumped."

"No, but they were experienced riders."

"All the more reason for me to do this myself. I *can* do this," Jim declared.

She motioned for him to go ahead and climbed back up on the corral fence. The man was as obstinate as a mule with an attitude!

"Now look, you candidate for a dog food factory,"

Jim growled at Duke, his brows drawn together. He stood hip shot with the hand holding the reins hooked by its thumb in his front pocket. He spoke with determination, but in the kind of firm yet quiet voice she'd said would get the horse's attention without spooking him. "I'm climbing up there whether you like it or not. Got it?"

Duke shook his head and snuffled. Crystal chuckled at the big gelding's shenanigans, and Jim shot her a quelling glare that had her laughing aloud. She saw him fighting a grin and liked him all the more for his sense of humor.

This time when he got into position he was too quick for Duke and was soon towering over the corral. "Now what?" he asked, patting Duke and taking the sting out of his earlier dog-food reference.

"First, there's your seat to address."

Jim glanced behind himself at the floor of the saddle and grinned. "You want to discuss my seat, huh?"

Crystal rolled her eyes. Maybe she didn't like his sense of humor, after all. "If I don't, you won't be able to walk tomorrow. Sit deep in the saddle. Knees slightly bent, knees and thighs rolled slightly in so the flat of your knee is against the saddle. Slightly arch your lower back and try to flex with Duke's movements. Shoulders square and even. Upper back erect. Sitting tall in the saddle isn't just a silly Hollywood myth."

She continued with hands-on instruction about how he should hold his lower body, legs and feet. And desperately tried to ignore the electric charge she felt just touching his body clinically. No one had ever accused her of being faint of heart so she continued, lengthening his stirrups and yanking his heels downward so they were lower than his toes and so that the balls of his feet were all that were in the stirrups. All the while she marveled that he didn't seem to hear her heart thundering.

"Now, don't keep your elbows so rigid. Relax them and keep them close to your sides. Keep your reining hand close at the pommel." She stepped back, surveying his form and giving herself a little breathing room. "You want to walk him a bit or have you had it for today?" she asked, hoping he wanted to call it a day.

She needed to get farther away where she could think. Jim Lovell was messing up her already-muddled mind. But she was doomed to disappointment.

"No sense in going through all that trouble getting up here and learning to sit right if I still can't ride," he said.

And Crystal wanted to scream.

Instead she smiled and prayed it didn't look like a grimace. "Oh-key-dokey," she said, trying to sound cheerful. "We'll learn how to start and stop our animal next."

Jim shot her a crooked grin and her pulse tripled. "Who's we? Ya' got a mouse in your pocket?" he teased in that distinctive, eastern city-boy accent of his, his brown eyes twinkling beneath the brim of his now-dusty red Phillies baseball cap. Maybe she'd get him a straw Stetson. He was a man who should wear a white hat even if he did have a smart mouth.

"Smart mouth, now *you're* going to learn how to start and stop, so listen up. There are four, what we call, natural aids that you'll use to tell your horse what you want him to do. Your hands, your voice, your legs and your weight."

She explained how best to use those natural aids, and Jim was soon able to start Duke moving forward at will and stop on command, as well. Then she moved to steering, explaining that with the reins in his left hand as she'd shown him to hold them, he should move that hand up the horse's neck, pulling lightly across Duke's neck in the direction he wanted the horse to go.

"Not quite like learning to steer my Mustang, but not much different." He cocked his head to the side, holding her gaze. "In fact, I think I'm learning how to steer Duke faster than I did Ruby. Maybe because you're a lot prettier than my dad was," he told her with a playful smile and a wink that made her heart turn over.

Unaccountably flattered, she felt as if she were standing in quicksand and every minute in his company had her sinking faster—deeper. Crystal told herself she was being ridiculous. After all, she'd apparently only eclipsed an aging veteran cop in his estimation.

Crystal told Jim to walk Duke around the corral in circles for a while and instructed him how to direct the big gelding in a half-circle reverse move. Once the two were moving around the ring in a good synchronous rhythm, she retreated to the fence, hoping to settle her heart and mind.

Lord, after all these years of being a loner, why am I so attracted to this man? He's sure to go back east. He'll miss his job soon. Writing won't feed the spirit I sense in him. Philadelphia, Pennsylvania. He'll be so far removed from my world, it's ridiculous. What is it about him? She paused, waiting for a definitive answer. None came just then. *You're not going to answer that, are You? You've already told me and I'm not hearing You, huh?*

After a while of watching, thinking and listening for the Lord's voice, Crystal called out instructions for Jim to stop Duke, start forward again, then to execute several half-circle reverses. Soon, both he and the animal seemed accustomed to giving and taking orders. And by then, she knew she had to get away from the sight of him "sitting tall in the saddle." The man looked as if he'd been born up there.

"I think that's all for today," she called out, and hopped down into the corral.

"That's all?" Jim looked disappointed.

"You're a fast learner, but we want to break you in, not break you. You *do* want to walk tomorrow, don't you?"

"Oh, definitely. I still have to learn how to gallop."

"First you learn to trot. Then you learn to gallop."

"Ah. Learn to walk before you run, grasshopper?" Jim said. "A wise woman once gave me that advice. My mother."

How was a woman supposed to resist a man who moved like a tiger, was drop-dead handsome and who was comfortable quoting his mother? She was doomed.

Chapter Nine

Evan Alton saw Jim Lovell sitting on the small stone porch in front of the cabin. He'd wanted to talk to him all day, but true to his word, Lovell had stuck like glue to Cris from late morning till now. He'd heard her go into the office and power up her computer a few minutes ago so this was the perfect opportunity for a little chat with his daughter's new protector.

"Got a minute?" he called as he approached the cabin he hadn't ventured inside of since Martha's death.

Lovell looked up from his laptop. "Sir?" he asked politely.

"I saw you and my daughter down at the corral earlier." They'd looked good together, his Cris and this big man. None of the men in the area seemed to appreciate her beauty. It was as if they couldn't look past her height and her solid build. Sure, she wasn't the delicate flower her mother had been, but she was a beauty all the same.

Lovell had certainly noticed, unless Evan had misunderstood the long looks he'd observed. Maybe he'd be staying on permanently. A man could write anywhere. And if that wasn't enough to keep a man like Jim Lovell busy, their sheriff needed replacing. Unfortunately, an awful lot of people didn't seem to be able to look past Caleb Hart's past. Which would make a former state policeman's job of getting elected real easy.

"Crystal was showing me my way around a horse," Lovell explained. "Apparently she won't be able to stay around the homestead, where she'd be safer, so I'll have to ride out with her."

Evan ignored the veiled censure he heard in the man's voice. That the Circle A was shorthanded couldn't be helped. Evan had long kept cost down and profits high by hiring hard workers and only as many as he absolutely needed.

"Did you enjoy riding Duke? You looked pretty good up there."

Lovell chuckled. "Yeah. Right. Like I was born in the saddle. Did you happen to see Duke dragging me off my feet?"

Evan laughed. "Missed that but I've seen it a time or two since Jackson left."

Memories coursed through him of the son he had feared he'd lost, until Jackson had finally called a few hours earlier. His son had actually sounded surprised when Evan told him he loved him. He fought off a wave of depression. Jackson would get over his little rebellion and come on home. Evan had to believe that because Martha would be sorely disappointed in him if he wasn't able to repair the damage his lie had caused to his relationship with their son.

And that was what it came right down to. He'd always meant to tell Jackson about his adoption even though, from the beginning, Evan had been against caving in to the biological mother's stipulations in that regard. Still, he'd promised Martha he'd fulfill the terms of the contract and find the right time to tell the boy. But no time had ever felt right.

Putting it off had begun with her illness. Then it had felt wrong to tell him after Martha's death. So soon after losing his mother, Evan had feared Jackson would feel he had no one if he learned Evan wasn't his father. Then as time went on and Evan's grief seemed to swallow him, he and the children grew apart. He wasn't blind. He knew his emotional distance affected his children. Cris was saddened by it and Jackson was angered, but that hadn't been enough to pull Evan out of the morass of pain that had swallowed him.

So before he'd seen it coming, the very real possibility had arisen that the boy would get into trouble to show his resentment of Evan. By the time he'd realized his son was too committed a Christian to act out his anger in misdeeds, Evan had worried that the strong young man Jackson had become would go in search of his real parent.

Though it hadn't happened until he was fully an adult, that was exactly what Jackson had done when the truth had accidentally come out. And now that he'd found his biological family, Evan guessed it was up to the Lord whether Jackson remained in Pennsylvania or came home to accept the legacy Evan continued to try to build for him.

"Is everything all right?" Lovell asked, startling Evan out of depressing thoughts.

Evan realized he not only had been staring off into space, but he'd been scowling, as well. He took off his hat and wiped the perspiration off his forehead with his sleeve before replacing the hat.

"I guess I'm just surprised Cris didn't warn you about Duke's little habit. You're a guest here. If you'd been hurt..." he explained, hoping to cover up his distraction.

"I'm not a guest. I'm a tenant. One who's getting free riding lessons. I think I'll survive having my dignity dented in front of your men."

Evan's heart lightened just a bit. Lovell had just jumped to Cris's defense. It was a promising sign. "I wouldn't worry about that. To a man they all got the same treatment. Duke's an equal-opportunity prankster. Got dumped by him myself earlier in the week." He rubbed his still-sore hip. "Listen, I wanted to thank you again for looking out for my daughter. I worry. You understand?"

Lovell nodded. "I'd worry, too. Don't kid yourself. This guy means business."

"Then I wasn't overreacting with King. I'd hoped—" Evan shook his head and let out a tired sigh as he shoved his hands in his back pockets. "Just between you, me and the fence post, I'm not too comfortable with Joe King conducting this investigation.

He's not taking this seriously. I think he ran for sheriff because it looked like a cushy job. It never occurred to the bozo that the county was quiet because Barrett worked hard to keep it that way.

"Anyway, I wondered if you could look over his shoulder a little. Make sure he does everything he should to protect Cris and find this maniac."

Lovell nodded, his expression showing the disgust with King that Evan felt. "Did you know he's asked Crystal out a few times and she sent him packing?"

Evan raised an eyebrow at that news. "Hadn't heard that."

"I heard you had to light a fire under him to get the evidence from last night sent up to the state lab."

"You thinking he's acting odd? Maybe guilty? Cris said the note made it sound as if she'd rejected this guy."

"That doesn't mean intentionally. It could be someone who's never even approached her. Loving her from afar, so to speak. But I can't rule King out especially since he seems to want to ignore the whole problem," Lovell said with an eloquent shrug. "So, yeah. I'll be happy to look over his shoulder. Could spice up the whole vacation."

He grinned. It was a cat-that-ate-the-canary kind of grin. It gave Evan the idea that Jim Lovell planned on toying with a certain incompetent sheriff while trying to end this thing safely for Cris.

"Good to hear. I'm doubly in your debt. Thanks again," he told the easterner, nodded then turned away.

He almost sighed aloud again, but this time in relief. With Lovell looking out for Cris, Evan could turn his mind fully back toward the Circle A, his beloved Martha's legacy to their children.

He looked around on his way to the corral where Tomas held an already saddled Apple Boy. The Circle A had changed and grown over the years, but there were things that Martha would remember if she could see the homestead now. The house, barn and distant scenery hadn't changed a bit. The changes were in the amount of land he now held, the number of head of cattle that land could support, the number of cowhands he could afford to hire and the fleet of five pickups that had replaced the beat-up old '59 Ford half-ton he'd had when they got married. There was, of course, the new stable and corrals in the distance, Jackson's own contribution to his own legacy. Martha would be so proud of the son she'd adored and of her beloved ranch.

When she'd renamed the ranch for a wedding gift, Evan had vowed to preserve and expand the Circle A's holdings, and he'd done just that. Keeping that vow was all that mattered to him in these past years. All that had kept him going.

Jim watched Evan Alton pace away toward Tomas who held a waiting horse down at the corral. He doubted the man would be as willing to hand his daughter into Jim's care if he'd been able to read Jim's mind a few hours earlier when he'd been with Crystal in that corral.

Jim didn't even trust himself. When she'd let out that laugh in the midst of his power struggle with the recalcitrant Duke, he'd thought his spine had turned to water and his thoughts had gone to places where he never let his mind wander.

Why did she affect him like this? He didn't seriously date. Occasionally, he'd share a meal with an interesting woman, but never with one he was attracted to because attraction just didn't happen to him anymore.

At least not before Crystal.

He'd been beyond feeling attraction since Jessie's death. For the most part, Jim didn't even notice women as women. They were people who interested him on an intellectual level.

But when Crystal had grabbed his knee to push it inward toward the horse, and when she'd put her hand on the small of his back to urge an arch into it, he'd been sincerely worried she'd hear his heart pounding and prayed fervently for the physical reactions her touch sent zinging through his body to go away.

He was still waiting!

If he didn't know better, he'd swear Cole Taggert had arranged this whole scenario to drive him slowly out of his mind. It would be the perfect payback for suspecting Cole in the arson and other problems at Laurel Glen last summer.

The worst part of this attraction was that it was more than the physical. She touched him in other, more emotional and spiritual ways than even Jessie had. When she'd glared at her laughing crew and tried to protect his ego by stepping in to help, it had affected his heart as much as her touch had made it pound. And that was trouble with a capital *T*.

He was there to find the truth about her brother, but worry over her welfare and emotions had moved to the forefront of his concern. All she had to do was look unhappy when Jackson's name came up and he let her change the subject rather than push for answers. And heaven forbid if she discovered his true mission in Colorado. Just the thought had made him feel complete and utter panic and robbed him of speech.

He'd nearly swallowed his tongue earlier when she asked if he'd heard stories about violent horses. Into his mind had burst the story of Cole's mother and her tragic violent death beneath the hooves of her son's fifteenth birthday gift. Jim had panicked, thinking she knew of his connection to Laurel Glen. Of his mission in Colorado. But after he'd stammered pitifully for a few seconds he'd gotten a hold of his runaway panic. Knowledge of an incident that infamous in the Philadelphia area could easily be chalked up to coincidence.

And a coincidence was exactly what it once had been. Years before he'd ever considered taking a job with the state police or before he'd been assigned to investigate the vandalism at Laurel Glen, Jim had indeed heard about how Marley Taggert had died from the responding state police officer. He hadn't needed to lie to Crystal about that, at least.

For the first time, Jim understood how his friend Greg had felt years ago during an undercover mission when he'd been forced to lie to the woman he'd fallen in love with. Luckily for Jim, he didn't intend to love Crystal. Love and relationships—lasting or short-term—were not for James Reed Lovell. No way. No how.

He would not get in any deeper with Crystal. He would guard her and help solve this case as a form of preemptive penance for the false pretenses of his presence. After that, he'd move on to uncover Jackson Alton's motives. And Crystal's life wouldn't be the only thing being guarded.

Jim intended to guard his heart most of all.

"You know, you're pretty nosy for a visitor," King said, nearly overbalancing his desk chair as he leaned back and propped his boots on the desk. It was a ploy to make him look relaxed, but Jim could see past the lazy body language to the anger in King's face and in his clenched hand.

He was really getting on King's nerves. Torrence's incompetent sheriff was on the verge of a snit, and it was a lot more fun watching him try to hide it than watching a sitcom.

Jim grinned. He knew his next volley would hit its mark. "Evan Alton asked me to look in on your progress but, if it bothers you, I can always conduct my own private investigation. Everyone around here seems to think highly of Crystal. I'm sure they'd be glad to cooperate."

"You have no business meddling in this!" the sheriff shouted, bouncing up in his chair and pounding his feet into the floor.

"Evan asked me to protect his daughter and that makes it my business."

Now both King's hands were clenched into fists.

"He has no right to subvert my authority. The Altons have been a thorn in my side for years."

Jim didn't bother to try hiding the smirk he felt twisting at his mouth. "I heard something about that somewhere around town. Goes all the way back to eighth grade, I understand. Right? Jackson, a fifth-grader at the time, beat the daylights out of you for teasing his sister."

"That was kid stuff. I'm talking recent history. Alton's been buying up land around the Circle A. The Flying K was the biggest ranch in these parts till my brother let Alton intimidate him out of bidding for that land."

Jim was tired of trading veiled insults and listening to probably unfounded allegations. He leaned the heels of his hands on the desk and glared down at King. "Look, I don't care how much land your family controls. Or the Altons control. Or how many times Jackson Alton put you in your place or made a fool of you. Or if Crystal Alton turned you down when you asked her out. I care about her being terrified and in danger. If you aren't going to follow up leads, then I am. Got it?"

"I'm still the duly elected sheriff around here. I do as I please. You got *that?*"

As far as threats went, Jim was only a little worried. But the man's refusal to take Crystal's stalker seriously *was* a worry. No one was this stupid or complacent. Was he more than just lazy or pigheaded?

Was he guilty?

Chapter Ten

Thinking again about the sheriff's veiled threat, Jim smiled. Only a fool would take the grin a friend had once described as lethal for a friendly gesture. And he didn't think King was as big a fool as most people thought.

"You're not just the sheriff around here," he told the heavy man behind the desk. "You're something really special. You want to know what that is? You're the only one on my current list of suspects. And your reluctance to investigate this isn't changing my mind, Joey boy."

"Is there a problem?" Crystal asked from behind him, peeking in the doorway that led to the street.

Jim smoothed out his features and straightened. Turning halfway toward her, he propped his hip on the edge of King's desk. "No problem at all. I was just telling the sheriff that I understand how short-handed he is and how ill prepared his small-town office is to deal with your sort of problem. He's going to get that line tap ordered and follow up on the paint and chrome pieces with the state lab. Then he'll be putting out an APB in the surrounding counties for any car sporting front-end damage that matches whatever make and model the lab tells him they've narrowed our parameters to include.

"And I've promised to help out by sitting down this afternoon and alerting every body shop in a hundred-mile radius to report any white or silver cars that come in with damage to their front quarter panel. I'll be stopping by again, *Sheriff*, to see if you need help with anything else."

"You do that," King snarled.

Jim didn't comment further. He just pivoted the rest of the way toward the door, pushed off the desk, which sent it sliding into King's round belly. Jim joined Crystal on the sidewalk in front of the small storefront jailhouse. He grinned at the *oomph* sound behind him as King tried to regain his breath.

"I thought buildings like that only existed in old TV shows and movies," he remarked to Crystal, hoping to divert her from the scene she'd interrupted.

The sun made her silky waist-length hair shimmer as it ruffled in the soft breeze. It looked like a waterfall in the moonlight. She smiled up at him, but the look in her eyes warned him that she wasn't going to be diverted.

"Sheriffs like Joe King usually only exist in Hollywood's wild imagination, too. You, sir, were tilting at windmills in there."

Jim decided to play dumb. "How so?"

"You were trying to get him to really investigate those calls and the accident."

"It wasn't an accident and he'll investigate because he knows if he doesn't, I will. And I let him know that so far there's only one person in town looking guilty. Him."

"You were serious when Caleb was out at the ranch earlier." Crystal stopped walking and turned to him. "I don't like Joe King. Or think much of him. But this?"

"I'm not settling on him alone. But he does fit the motive in that note," Jim said as he looked around to get his bearings. "You rejected him and you can't think of anyone else. I need to get over to the library so I can look up the names and numbers of those body shops."

Crystal nodded and turned to cross the street, heading toward the library building. "So you're calling the body shops. What's next after that?"

Jim wished he knew. Wished there was more he could do besides stay near her and watch for the next thing to happen. "I wish I could get this in front of a profiler."

"I suppose Sheriff King would be a real stumbling block there. Budget, you know. I guess Dad and I could kick in the fee. Do you really think it could help?"

Would it? "I honestly don't know. We only have one note and…actually you've told me very little about the phone calls. I don't even know the pattern."

"At first, there was no one on the other end if my father answered. The line would just go dead. For the first few days my father thought it was Jackson so he stopped answering. I picked up the phone after that, thinking maybe Dad was right and that Jackson hadn't wanted to talk to him. But whoever it was stayed on the line, just breathing. Listening.'' She shuddered. "It gave me the creeps, but I thought it was a prank. So did my father.''

Jim pulled a notebook out of his back pocket. "When about was that?'' he asked.

"Actually I know the date. The first call came on the Fourth of July.''

Jim wrote as he walked, something he'd mastered years ago. "How long did that pattern last?''

"A week. No. Till the following Sunday night. I remember because Julia and I went to dinner in Greeley between the morning and evening services. That was the night he started saying he loved me and wished he was with me. At two a.m. it was pretty clear where I was at the time. That lasted for about two weeks. Then he—'' Her voice broke. They were near the library by then and Jim took her arm leading her to a bench under the tree near the stone front steps.

"Try to calm down. You just went seven shades of pale. He's not going to get to you.''

Crystal nodded, looking at the ground. Her long waterfall of hair dropped forward over her shoulder, obscuring her face. Taking the excuse it provided, Jim swallowed and reached out, smoothing it back over her shoulder. Just as he'd imagined, it felt like strands of deep dark silk.

"Thanks for being here. For trying so hard to help," she said, still avoiding his gaze.

He grinned. "Just part of the job, ma'am."

She glanced his way, offering him a small, chagrined smile. "I don't usually fall apart this way."

"Your world's been invaded. An invisible evil is casting a shadow over your life. You have a right to fall apart once or twice a day. I hate to push you but if I'm going to work up a profile on this guy, I need to know where he went after he got tired of innuendo? To specifics."

She looked away. Nodded. "I can't—"

He covered her hand. "I don't need the exact words. Just tell me if I'm right. Okay?" She nodded again. "He started cataloging his fantasies where you're concerned."

Her head moved almost imperceptibly up and down. He wrote down her affirmative answer. "How long before he started to threaten?"

"About two weeks. Then last Tuesday night—well, I guess technically it was Wednesday morning—he called all night until I threatened to have my lines tapped. He hasn't called since."

"No, now he escalated early."

"Early? You mean there was a pattern until he left the note and pushed me off the road."

Oddly, Crystal didn't know how she felt about the fact that her threat had pushed this guy into action. As frightening as Thursday night had been, at least now once she was asleep no phone calls woke her. Although falling asleep the last two nights hadn't been very easy.

Jim covered her hand. Until then she'd been clutching the seat of the bench in a death grip, but his touch instantly relaxed her.

"He's growing angrier. And scary as that is, it might mean he'll get careless," Jim explained.

She looked at him, so strong, so solid and calm. "So in a strange way this could be encouraging?"

Jim nodded. "What do you say we go look up those numbers?"

Crystal stood to follow, her mind still in a partial fog. But Jim put his hand at the small of her back, encouraging her to walk just half a step in front of him, snapping her mind into instant awareness of herself and her surroundings. Jim made the time she spent with him different from any time she'd spent with any other man. He had old-fashioned courtly manners, as did many of her male friends, but none of them had ever used them on her.

"Hold up a minute. You forgot your bag," he said, and walked the few step back to the bench. He returned, holding the bag out to her.

Crystal smiled. She'd wondered when the right time would be to give him his gift. She didn't have to wonder any longer. He already had it so she made no move to take the bag when he held it out to her. Confusion immediately wrote itself on his features.

"Aren't you going to ask what's in it?" she asked him.

"No way. I have a sister. Remember? Ask a question like that and you just might be sorry if you get the answer."

"It's for you. Open it."

He took out the white straw Stetson and stared at it. "Th-thanks. I… Why?"

"Congratulations on learning to ride. You have to have the right hat to ride with us Monday. Put it on. If it doesn't fit they'll help you pick one out that does over at Bunny Junction."

He took off the Phillies cap and stuffed the peak in his back pocket. "Bunny Junction?" he asked, and fit the hat to his head.

Above him on the first step, she checked the fit. It was perfect. "It's the clothes store. They specialize in work clothes, Western-style shirts, tack, boots. That sort of thing."

Jim glanced around at the few people on the street and chuckled. "They must do a land-office business around here. That's all anyone wears. All the men anyway."

Crystal looked down at her boots, jeans, snap-front shirt. "And me," she said just a tad brusquely. Not a minute ago he'd made her feel like a lady and now she was just one of the guys again. It stung!

Jim's smile didn't dim. "I know," he said, his tone admiring and appreciative. "A walking advertisement for Bunny Junction is what you are. They should pay you. I can't imagine why, to a woman, the women in this town haven't seen you dressed like that and fol-lowed suit. Talk about competition."

Crystal laughed. "You're ridiculous. Men like dainty flowers the way my mother was. Ruffles and bows."

Jim stepped up next to her and shook his head. "Your education has been sadly stifled in this town.

I'm a man and little, skinny women scare me. One good hug and you've broken something. Nope. The guys around here are dopes.'' He slung his arm around her shoulders and started up the steps. ''Idiots,'' he continued. ''Dolts. Dummies,'' he went on, adding a disparaging name with each one step.

Crystal couldn't stop laughing once they burst into the library.

''Shh,'' Julia hissed. Then her eyes brightened and her annoyance smoothed out when she saw who it was. ''Crystal, what on earth is going on?''

''Sorry. My guard dog here has a weird sense of humor,'' Crystal explained.

''One you seem to enjoy.'' Julia smiled broadly.

''I thought you were staying the weekend with your aunt?''

''She'd planned to take a bus trip to Denver with the seniors' group she belongs to. She forgot about it until I spotted it on her calendar and made her go. Now, tell my why you'd call this nice man a guard dog?''

Oh! No. Julia had gone to visit her aunt on Friday morning so Crystal hadn't told her about what had happened, afraid to spoil her fun. She knew her friend would be horrified. But now that she'd slipped, there was little she could do about it. ''I had an accident on the way home on Thursday night.''

''It wasn't an accident,'' Jim muttered from behind her.

''How could it not be an accident?'' Julia asked, clearly confused.

Crystal glared at Jim before answering. ''You were

right about the phone calls, Jule. There *is* someone stalking me. Somehow he stole my cell phone and put a threatening note in its place in my purse. Then he ran me off the road on my way home from town.''

Julia backed up as a look of shock took over her pretty features. She looked as if she might crumple to the floor. Jim rushed around the tall counter and guided her into a chair. Crystal had expected Julia to be upset, but she hadn't expected her gentle friend to practically faint dead away.

She followed Jim around the counter and crouched down next to Julia. ''I'm so sorry. I didn't mean to frighten you.'' Crystal looked up at Jim. ''The phone books are on the back wall, I think. Could you give us a few minutes?''

Backing away and looking a little panicked himself, Jim said, ''Take all the time you need. I can handle looking up the phone numbers.'' His grimace told her he couldn't handle Julia falling apart so completely. Crystal almost smiled, but Julia's distressed voice bled away any enjoyment Jim's consternation brought her.

''What happened?'' her mild friend nearly sobbed as Jim fled the check-out station. ''And who *is* he? I thought he was a writer renting the cabin.''

''He is. He's also a Pennsylvania State Police detective on vacation. After the accident, Dad asked Jim to watch out for me.''

''Watch out for you? Oh! The guard dog reference.''

''And he's awfully good at it. Personally, I don't

think he'll be happy as a writer. He's too good a cop. You should see him in action.''

''How so?''

''Joe King—sheriff extraordinaire—didn't want to come out to the wreck so Jim told Mirabel he'd personally secure the scene while we waited. And he did.'' She went on to describe all Jim did at the scene before the local law arrived. ''Joe and Caleb came right out, of course.'' Crystal went on grinning. ''Jim said they would and they did, but he had everything handled already.''

Julia's hand fluttered then settled on her chest. ''My goodness. He sounds like a superhero.''

Crystal didn't try to fight the silly grin that tugged at her mouth. ''At least a supercop. He's even agreed to help out around the Circle A since we're short a man without Jackson.''

''Crystal, speaking of Jackson, it's time you called him home. Surely you see you need him.''

''My brother has his own problems to deal with right now. Besides which, I don't need him. I have Jim now. Honestly, I've never felt safer than I do with him nearby. Jule, I've never felt…''

''I hope you aren't falling in love with him. He's a city man.'' Julia gripped Crystal's shoulder, surprising her with her strength. ''Crystal, he's going to leave.''

''Maybe I'll go with him.''

''Go with— You'd hate it where he's from. Besides, he could be killed and leave you all alone. I never want you to feel the kind of pain I did when my parents were killed. Look at how dangerous even his vacations are!''

Crystal chuckled. ''You could get a job as a professional worrier. Jim can take care of himself *and* me. I have nothing to worry about.''

Chapter Eleven

Crystal watched Jim and Duke double back to head off a steer and turn him in the right direction. In the last two weeks, her volunteer bodyguard had become a passably good cowhand. He couldn't rope to save his life, but Duke obeyed his silent commands and—more important—Jim had learned when to let the horse take over the work of directing the cattle.

Her feelings for him were a growing worry, though. The roundup she'd dreaded had turned out to be fun because she'd experienced it through new eyes. She had enjoyed watching him learn and conquer each new aspect of the life she lived. But what of *his* life? It was never far from her mind that he'd put his dreams on hold for her.

They'd ridden home at night the first week, driving the cows to new areas where water was plentiful. But since then they'd been working outlying sections of the ranch and had camped. In those early days she supposed if Jim had any energy left he'd been able to write, but this last week that hadn't been possible. Coward that she was, she hadn't asked.

Her father had her worried, too. What was going on with him? He'd left her and the crew two days ago, saying he had an appointment in Denver. It was totally unlike him. This roundup had been his idea, so why would he schedule a meeting in the middle of it? Crystal had never questioned his recent trips to the city, but now she realized they'd become frequent and almost had a pattern to them. As if he had appointments. With a doctor? Jim had laughingly speculated on the existence of a secret woman, but Crystal knew her father. No one would ever come before the ranch and his grief over the loss of her mother. Not even his own children. Certainly not another woman.

He and Duke directed the recalcitrant steer into the makeshift corral they'd constructed. Jim trotted over to her, wearing a smile as sunny as the day. Relaxed on horseback now, he leaned his forearm on the pommel. "That's about it. Cal and Harry said to tell you that mother and calf were all they found on their sweep."

"Jerry and Mike just checked in," she told him. "They didn't find anything in their search area. I guess that's it. I have to think you'll be glad. You came out here to write and you haven't written a word in at least the last week. You're wasting your vacation working."

"Nothing we ever do in life is a waste. I've learned so much about a different way of life. It's been restful in its own way."

She laughed. "Oh, real restful. In the saddle from

dawn till dinner, eating dust, slapping at flies, fighting smelly steaks on the hoof. I think the sun fried your brain. You need a vacation from your vacation.''

Jim stared at her solemnly. ''It wasn't a vacation, remember. It was a leave of absence. If I hadn't done it—'' He looked away.

''It's still eating at you. Jim, what happened?''

His eyes narrowed. Not in anger but thought. ''Being a cop back east isn't like the job Joe King holds. It can be dirty. Thankless. Futile. Years ago I got into a shoot-out with a guy robbing my local bank branch. I was off duty. Cashing my paycheck. He pulled a gun and so did I. When it was all over I'd stopped the robbery and the robber was dead. Then we pulled off his ski mask. He was a kid. Fifteen years old.''

''Oh, Jim.'' Her heart went out to him. ''That was too young to die, but you didn't send him into that bank.''

''No. Poverty did. Not just poverty of the wallet but of the spirit. I thought I'd gotten over it. Left it back there in Riverside with all the rest of the stuff I wanted to put behind me. Remember I mentioned the shooting that started me questioning why I'd become a cop?''

''How could I forget something like that? You were nearly killed.''

''Yeah. There was a huge drug raid planned in Chester. It's a really depressed little city so they needed the added manpower. The mayor asked for state police support. Since I'd once worked drugs undercover I was asked to go along with some troopers and a couple of other detectives. The long and the short of it is that I wound up standing in an alley behind the building facing a kid with a gun. I don't know where my mind went. One second I saw his face and the next a bullet whizzed by my head. Training took over, I guess. I dropped as more slugs hit the wall next to me. Then a shot came from off to my left and the kid was falling to the ground. One of the detectives I traveled there with had fired when I hadn't.''

"How long were you...?" she paused, not knowing what to call his lapse. It worried her. She knew he belonged on the force, but she hadn't really pictured him as being in harm's way.

"How long was I zoned out? Maybe five seconds. Beginning to end, the whole incident took maybe fifteen seconds. But that's all it takes. It's why I needed this time away from everything familiar. If I can't stay focused, I can't do the job. Now that your father won't take rent because I'm watching out for you, I can afford to extend the leave. So don't worry about time. I'm not.

"Believe me, this has been an incredible experience. People pay for opportunities like this." He gestured to the distant horizon. "Just look around you."

She did and saw the same thing she'd been seeing her whole life. She'd never been farther from home than Denver. There was a world out there and she'd seen none of it.

"Are we drivin' these cows the rest of the way in today?" the walkie-talkie at her hip squawked.

Crystal checked her watch and pulled the device off her hip. "That's what Dad wanted and I guess there's time. I'd like an hour more of daylight, but with luck we'll make it before sunset."

"I can't say I'm sorry," Jim said, and shifted in the saddle looking a little uncomfortable. "Like I said, it was an experience but—"

"So is root canal, but who volunteers for that?" Crystal finished for him. He'd been a good sport but if she, a person who loved the ranch, hated this kind of work, Jim had to be fed up with it. "Let's get this over with. Okay, guys. Let's get these dogies headed for water," she said into the walkie-talkie then grinned at Jim.

"Gee, I love that kind of talk," he said, and waited expectantly for her to identify the vintage TV line. It had become a game between them. He was winning.

"Chuck Parker. *McHale's Navy*. But you missed my line," she taunted.

"No, I didn't. Rowdy Yates. *Rawhide*," he shot over his shoulder as he and Duke took off after the first of the herd to break ranks.

Two hours later, Jim watched Crystal cut to the right of a steer trying to make a break for it. She expertly drove the steer back to the herd. She and Lady were Western poetry in action.

He scanned the area. Then, satisfied that she was safe, he took a moment just to watch her. She'd become important to him, and he couldn't leave until he was sure she was safe. If he learned tomorrow what Jackson Alton's motive was for hiding his past when he took the job at Laurel Glen, he'd still have to stay on.

For the next two hours, Crystal showed Jim how to patrol the edges of the large herd and how to encourage stragglers to move on and keep with the crowd. When a mama and baby veered out of the herd at a dried-up stream, Jim kicked Duke into high gear and gave chase. After failing miserably to turn the stubborn pair toward the herd and knowing the mama would follow her calf, he got ready to bend down to slip a rope over the calf's head. It was the only way he could get a rope on anything, having entertained the Circle A cowhands and the Altons for the last two weeks with his truly terrible efforts at roping.

Smiling, he dipped down in the saddle to hook the calf. A shot rang out, tearing into his upper arm. A second whizzed by his ear, and instinct took over. Jim kicked loose of the stirrups and dove into the dry creek bed over the back of the calf. Holding his bleeding arm, he scrambled against the bank, using it for cover. A third shot burrowed through the bank, driving into the creek bed and narrowly missing his leg. Jim scrambled back and tried to get his bearings.

Since the loose dirt of the bank wasn't enough to stop a bullet and Jim knew the shooter had his location, he crawled, cradling his aching arm against his chest. He hoped to get behind one of the cottonwoods growing along the creek.

Once there, he dropped his head against the tree roots and fought dizziness. Now that he was protected, he could get his head above the rim of the bank without getting it shot off. Gritting his teeth against the pain, he rolled over and pushed himself up the bank to search for Crystal. He had to make sure she was out of danger since he'd clearly become the target of the madman who'd been dogging Crystal.

A fourth shot pinged into the tree, keeping him pinned behind it. After a few frantic seconds, Jim was able to find her with the herd, but when he did, his heart stilled. Now he understood the distant tremor he felt in the earth. She stood in the saddle waving her arms directly in harm's path. Harm for her was in the form of a stampeding herd of panicked cattle running from the sound of the shots. His breath dammed in his lungs until, just before the frightened steers reached her, she and Lady swung away and turned to run with them.

Jim exhaled, fighting a dizziness either from blood loss or relief as he watched her safely galloping away in the midst of the herd. Out of sight but out of rifle range, too.

Confident that she was okay, Jim turned his attention to his situation. He looked around and found the only place the shots could have come from. The creek made a drastic ninety-degree turn about two hundred yards east of his position. It was heavy in ground cover and trees and the only place where a shooter could be hiding.

Unfortunately, Duke had also scrambled for safer territory, taking Jim's rifle with him. Frustrated, Jim looked around and took hold of a fallen branch with his right hand. It wasn't much of a weapon against a gun and what made it worse was, lamentably, he was a southpaw. But still, he had to try to flush this guy out.

Feeling naked without a firearm for protection, he started to crawl back in the direction he'd come when a new rumble in the earth drew his attention. It was coming closer. He rolled to his knees, ready to fight a deadly foe, but he quickly realized the clamor of hoofbeats and heaving breath came from the south.

Jim whipped around and blinked as Crystal, bent over in the saddle, rode along the creek bed toward him. "Are you crazy or trying to get yourself killed?" Without a thought to his own safety, he jumped up, reached for her and pulled her quickly to the ground with his good hand. He landed on his back and held her against his chest. Pain radiated down his arm, up across his shoulder and back.

"What did you think I'd do?" she demanded, trying to push away from him. Her gaze burned into his. "Run like a coward and not make sure you were okay back here?" Then alarm widened her eyes as they centered on his arm a few inches from her nose. "He shot you!"

He grinned. "Not meaning to sound clichéd but, 'It's just a flesh wound,'" he finished in an admittedly terrible English accent.

Her face crumpled. "*Monty Python and the Holy Grail.* The Black Knight. And this isn't funny," she cried. "You're bleeding all over the place."

Jim looked down. Okay, it was bleeding pretty heavily, but it wasn't serious. Jessie's wounds had been serious. Greg's had been serious. He'd seen serious and this wasn't it.

"Look, it hurts. A lot. But it really isn't that bad. The bullet just grazed me. Look," he said as he tore the material to expose the wound. Jim winced. The bullet had plowed a furrow nearly four inches long. It ran from about an inch above his elbow toward his shoulder before burrowing into the muscle. In the position he'd been in, had it not gone into the muscle, it would have hit his head.

Thank You, Lord, he prayed. *That was really close.* He looked at her. "I'll be fine. It could have been worse."

Crystal's lip trembled. "It could have killed you so easily. And it's worse than you thought. Isn't it?"

He nodded and yanked his shirt out of his jeans. "Rip off the tails, would you. We ought to get the bleeding stopped."

Crystal pulled out a pocket knife and went to work making a pad out of the two front sections. She then took the back and tied it tight around the wound.

Spots danced in front of his eyes when she tightened the tie on the makeshift bandage. He sucked a strangled breath, gritting his teeth. She would never know how close he came to passing out. This was not good. He had to get them out of there.

"Thanks. Still, you shouldn't have come back. You were safe with your men," he told her.

"This guy scares me, but I will not let him take away who I am."

"I…" Jim stopped. He understood. He wouldn't have left her, either. And he understood something else, something that ended his urgent worry. The shots had stopped. Using Lady's stirrup, he climbed cautiously to his feet and as quickly as possible pulled Crystal's rifle out of its holster on the saddle. Then he knelt back down on one knee in front of her using the rifle to hold himself up. He hooked the thumb of his left hand in the front belt loop to immobilize his injured arm.

"When you rode in, he didn't shoot at you and he didn't take the easy shot at me just now. I'm thinking he's gone. Stay here. I'm going over there to make sure it's safe," he said, pointing to the area where he thought the shots had originated.

"What if he comes here while you're there?" she asked. "And I don't think you could fire that rifle that's holding you up. Especially one-handed."

Jim stared at her then blinked. He wasn't thinking too straight. "Right. Fine. Come along but stay down and stay behind me. I'm supposed to be protecting you. Remember?" He handed the rifle to her.

She nodded and took the weapon, but grasped his hand. "He could have killed you."

"But he didn't. Admittedly it was close, but that only counts—"

"In horseshoes and hand grenades," she finished with a pained smile.

He grinned, trying to let her know he was all right. Her concern did funny things to him, but he didn't want to analyze it right then. He hadn't wanted her to care for him as much as she did. That, too, mixed up his emotions.

"Come on. Let's go see if we can pick up any clues. Remember, stay low and behind me."

Chapter Twelve

It didn't take long for Jim to confirm what he'd suspected from the second he'd landed in the creek bed. The shooter had hidden in the undergrowth around the recently dried-up creek. They'd all been sitting ducks, but this madman had singled out one lone writer-investigator-bodyguard. It didn't take a genius to know Crystal was the reason and not someone trying to prevent him from finishing the book he was supposedly there to write.

And that someone was a careful man. Very careful. The perp had even taken the time to pick up the shell casings and to dust out with a branch all the tracks he and his horse had made. The irregular pattern in the dust told the story of where the man had hidden, but it yielded no important clues. Jim was left with only educated speculation.

For instance, he had to assume the shooter had ridden away when Crystal galloped down the creek bed to Jim's rescue, which explained why he'd felt vibration from both directions. But the tall, hard-packed, drought-browned plain allowed for no hoof prints that might have been traceable.

With Crystal's help, Jim dug the slugs that had narrowly missed his leg out of the creek bed and the cottonwood. Then she went to round up Duke, leaving Jim leaning against the tree that had probably saved his life. Letting her go off on her own worried him, but since her stalker was clearly long gone from the area he thought it was safe. Prayed it was safe.

He was doing a lot of praying right then because he wasn't feeling too good and they had a long ride ahead. And though his head wasn't too clear, he knew air rescue would call attention to his injury and Crystal's added vulnerability. The way he figured it, the perp didn't know Jim had been hit and he wanted to keep it that way. Crystal was safer if the guy didn't learn her bodyguard was injured.

He decided to call Caleb Hart as soon as they got into cell range and have him meet them at the Circle A homestead. But right then he needed a doctor more than a cop. He hoped and prayed Caleb could get Doc Reynolds to come out to the Circle A to patch him up without involving King or alerting the clinic/town grapevine.

Having contacted her men, Crystal returned with Duke. She'd told them to start rounding up the cattle again and asked Ike Cannon to ride to the ranch house and give her a progress report in the morning.

The ride that followed a painful climb into Duke's saddle wasn't something he'd been looking forward to. And after those first jarring steps, he knew his imagination had been kind. About an hour's torturous ride put them in cell phone range and he called Caleb Hart. It was frustrating to have Caleb offer the air rescue he'd already decided to refuse, but if they were going to be keep his injury quiet, he had to ride in on Duke.

Crystal was never so glad to see the outline of the Circle A buildings come into view. Jim had said little, but she knew he was in considerable pain. She'd wanted to grab the cell phone from him and order Caleb to call the chopper. But no matter what she said, Jim persisted with his plan to hide his injury.

Nothing would ever erase the memory of hearing those shots ring out or of seeing Jim dive for cover into the dried-up creek bed. Or the memory of being pulled off Lady and into his strong arms. Or the horror she'd felt seeing his blood soaking his shirtsleeve.

Darkness was falling when they finally lumbered into the yard. Caleb stepped out of the barn to greet them, grabbing Duke's halter as he reached up to steady Jim. "You don't look so good, amigo," Caleb told him.

"I'll tell you, Deputy Hart, I've felt better on my worst day. Is Doc Reynolds here?" There was an edge of desperation in Jim's hoarse voice.

Caleb nodded. "He's up at the cabin waiting. You ready to get down from there?"

"Now there's a funny thing," Jim said with an exhausted grin on his pale face. "Since I got up here, getting down is about all I've been dreaming about, but that cabin looks a little too far to walk right now. Unfortunately, I think I'm just about...done in."

"Jim!" Crystal shouted as he slumped toward Caleb. She made a grab for him and caught his shirt in a death grip. The shoulder seam strained under his weight, but it held and so did she.

"I've got him!" Caleb grunted and somehow kept Jim in the saddle by practically laying him over Duke's neck. Duke sidestepped nervously, knocking into Caleb. "Cris, dismount and keep Duke calm. If we can get Jim up to the cabin on the horse, I can carry him inside. I think. He doesn't look any too light."

Remembering helping him into the saddle, she knew he wasn't. It didn't take long to get him into her brother's big bed, but each second was agonizing for her to watch. And all the time one thought kept going through her mind.

This is all my fault.

"He's a strong one. I'll say that," Doc Reynolds said about an hour later as he walked into the cozy parlor.

Crystal turned from the window and rushed across the room. "Should he be at the clinic? Say the word and I'll call the ambulance myself. I don't care who knows he's hurt." Nothing was as important as Jim right then. It was bad enough thinking of him leaving to go home, but dying? A world without that wicked sense of humor and teasing smile thriving somewhere in it? No. That she couldn't handle.

Gray-haired and bespectacled, Doc Reynolds was

the epitome of a small-town doctor. He'd known them all from the time they were in diapers and treated them accordingly. "You just calm down, missy. Sit," he ordered, pointing to the sofa. "Sit before you fall down. I don't need another patient. I told you he was going to be fine. He *is* fine," he reiterated.

"But he lost so much blood."

Reynolds raised one bushy gray eyebrow. "Are you doubting me?"

"But he was unconscious," she protested, gripping the cushion to keep from wringing her hands.

"Which came in handy getting him inside and getting that bullet out. The Good Lord was kind, so don't second-guess Him. Even with the local anesthetic, he'd have been in considerable pain while I worked on him."

That ride in rushed across her mind's eye. "He just kept getting worse. At first, after he had me bandage it, he was doing…okay. Not great but…"

Doc Reynolds pried the hand closest to him from the cushion and took it in his firm grip. "Cris, honey. This isn't Hollywood where the makeup people supply the blood and the hero keeps going like nothing happened. Getting shot is a shock to the body. Highly painful and traumatic. The blood pressure goes up or down depending on the person, and infection starts setting in quickly under the less-than-sterile conditions he was in. Then the body starts fighting that, too, and things go haywire again. It'll take a week or two of rest and antibiotics but he'll be right as rain. Good as new."

Crystal shook her head. "No. I saw that awful damage to his arm."

Reynolds nodded. "It wasn't pretty. I'll give you that, but I did a little fancy cutting and suturing. It would have been better done at the clinic, but I've been working in less than ideal conditions for years." He paused, then smiled kindly. "Don't you worry. It'll be a nice and neat scar and him being a man, it'll give him a springboard to a story that'll wow his friends back east. Now he just has to rest up a bit."

She tried to blink back the tears of relief that flooded her eyes, but lost the battle. When they spilled onto her cheeks, Doc Reynolds wiped them away with his handkerchief. "He's going to be okay," he said slowly as if speaking to a half-wit—which she admitted she was at that point—then he hugged her and said, "I promise, little girl. He'll be just fine." After one last squeeze he set her away from him. "Now, how about you? I want you to get some sleep."

She looked toward the bedroom. "But Jim needs—"

"Uh-uh-uh. No arguments, young lady. I've shot him full of pain medication. When he falls asleep, he'll be asleep for hours. I want you to go on up to the house, have some dinner, take a shower and climb into bed. Anna's waiting to baby you."

"But nothing happened to me."

"Don't try to buffalo your old doc. Your friend was shot, and you had to go through that ride with him. Now go in and smile real pretty for him, then skedaddle. I'm going to have some of that coffee and hit the road myself.''

Crystal bolted from the sofa and hurried into the master bedroom and slowed down just in time so she didn't look so anxious to see him. Which she was. And when she could see him, she was anxious for more. She longed to feel his arms around her. Longed for that kiss he'd almost given her the night they'd had dinner in town.

Caleb was sitting in a chair next to Jim, who was propped on several pillows. His muscular arm was bandaged from elbow to shoulder. So much damage. So much pain. And all her fault.

''I'm so sorry,'' she whispered.

Jim looked up, then his eyes cut to Caleb. ''Could we finish this in a few minutes?''

Caleb stood. ''I think that's enough for tonight. You both need some rest. I'll go get the slugs out of your saddlebags and get them up to the state lab. And thanks for trusting me. You won't be sorry. I'll be by in the morning after I talk to King.''

Jim nodded.

''Take care,'' Caleb said, and turned toward her and the doorway. ''Get some rest, Cris. You had a rough day.'' He touched her shoulder and left.

Crystal blinked. Had Doc Reynolds lied to her? Caleb seemed awfully worried. Frowning, she sat in the chair Caleb had vacated. ''Feeling any better?'' she asked Jim.

He stared at her, his eyes a little less than focused and a bit fevered. Finally he blinked and said, ''A lot. Your Doc Reynolds is quite a character. I came to while he was stitching me up. I got a long lecture for not letting you call in a chopper. I honestly never thought of the strain that ride put on · you." He reached up, running the tips of his fingers along her cheek. "Sometimes I get tunnel vision when I'm working on a case. Finding this nutcase is important to me. I don't want anything to happen to you."

Her cheek tingled and she was suddenly aware of her breathing. Again she found herself blinking back tears. Honestly, all she did lately was cry!

"I feel so guilty," she told him. "If it weren't for me, you wouldn't be hurt. You wouldn't have forced yourself to make that awful ride."

His gaze was less focused now than it had been just a couple minutes earlier. "Nah. That was all macho pride," he said in a slightly slurred voice, which she found terribly endearing. "Just don't want the guy to know he winged me." He gave her a sleepy, crooked grin. "I admit this carries method writing a little far but, hey. 'It's an adventure,'" he finished.

She rolled her eyes. "Are you ever serious?"

"Come on." With another sleepy grin he urged, "Who said it, and what movie?"

"I think the navy had it first."

"Movie. Character. I'm still one up on you. You admittin' defeat?"

"Never." Crystal forced herself to smile. "Chief Petty Officer Casey Ryback said it in *Under Siege.*" He had her smiling now, too. "If they hadn't edited it for TV you'd have had me on that one."

"No, I wouldn't. That's where I saw it." He shook

his head and dropped it back on the pillow. "What'd he give me?"

"Something to let you sleep." She leaned forward and did something she'd been dying to do for weeks. She brushed the hair off his forehead as he watched her with wide, unfocused, dark chocolate eyes. "Sleep," she told him.

He gave her a sleepy grin. "Don't think I have a choice." A frown wrinkled his forehead. "But I still need to tell you...uh...something. Can't remember. What'd he give me?"

"Sleep," she ordered softly again.

And this time, on a sigh, he did.

Late-morning light slanted across Crystal's eyes and sent her bolting straight up in bed. What was she doing in bed so far past dawn?

Then she remembered.

The shots. The stampede. Jim's bloody wound. That awful ride in.

She jumped out of bed. Someone should be taking care of him. *She* should be taking care of him! Dressing in record time, she tore through the house.

"Crystal!" Anna called just as she reached the side door nearest the cabin. We have company for breakfast. Where are you going in such a hurry?"

"I overslept. I have to look in on Jim."

"Then you should come to the breakfast table since he is our guest."

What is he doing out of bed!

"What are you doing out of bed?" she demanded as she rushed to the breakfast room.

"My arm took the hit, not my legs."

"But you were unconscious last night. If Caleb and I hadn't been there, you'd have done a header into the dirt."

He chuckled. "I have a friend. Big, tough ex-cop. The minister I told you about. When he cuts himself, he drops like a rock. Embarrassing but not fatal. Doc Reynolds was here at dawn. He gave me my orders and some pain pills. I'm fine. I can't move my arm a lot so eating isn't going to be pretty, but I already warned Anna that I'm a hopeless southpaw."

She eyed him. "Well, you do look better," she allowed, and sat across from him.

He nodded as he said, "There you go. I also talked to Caleb. We both think it would be a good idea if you rode out with Ike when he comes in. Since we know the person shooting at us wasn't one of your cowhands I—Caleb and I—" he corrected, "think you'd be safer with them right now."

Crystal nodded in response as Anna put their plates in front of them. At least if she was out with the men, rounding up the cattle again, Jim would not be the one protecting her, putting himself in danger for her. Because no matter what, she didn't want to be responsible for the death of the man she'd fallen asleep thinking about. The man she'd realized in the middle of a hail of bullets she loved more than life itself.

Chapter Thirteen

Jim pushed his laptop computer farther onto the dinette table, wondering where his head had gone. Nancy, his protagonist, had turned into a clone of Crystal; her green eyes and blond hair had morphed into eyes dark as obsidian and tresses black as a raven's wing. His sheriff had gained fifty or so pounds and for the last several chapters had looked suspicious—more like the villain than the hero of the piece. His chief suspect—the new guy in town—was trying to protect Nancy from an evil he didn't understand. None of his characters were doing what they were supposed to and hadn't been for the whole week! He'd written about thirty pages and deleted just as many. Why had he ever thought he wanted to be a writer?

He stood and stalked into the kitchen to pour himself some of Anna's iced tea. The Circle A's housekeeper had turned mother hen since the night he was shot when he'd awakened several times to find her sitting by his bed. She'd taken to supplying his every need and then some, grateful for his attempts to help Crystal.

Evan Alton purported to be grateful, as well, but he was so self-absorbed most of the time, it was hard to tell if he'd meant what he'd said. He'd returned from his trip about an hour after Crystal left with Ike. Truthfully, her father had seemed shaken by the shooting, but he'd still grumbled about pounds being run off his cattle by the stampede that followed the shots. Later the same day, Evan had ridden out to join Crystal and the men in their roundup effort.

And that left Jim with nothing to do. Unless it was to write a book that wanted to become a personal journal, and to mull over the disappointing news that the paint sample sent to the state lab couldn't have come from the same car as the trim.

Caleb couldn't explain it. He'd started out with two possibilities. Either the perp had dropped the trim to throw them off or the paint samples Caleb took from the pickup had been switched by King.

Then the deputy had quietly checked out the sheriff's alibi for the time of the shooting last Monday and that had gotten them nowhere except to dismiss a major theory. King had been with someone the entire time of the shooting. Although he'd at first claimed his horse had thrown a shoe, keeping him out of touch for longer than he'd expected.

When the Flying K's farrier had admitted the horse hadn't needed a shoe, Caleb had confronted his boss. King's day hadn't been spent innocently, but it had been spent with someone else—someone else's wife.

She'd reluctantly confessed, giving King an ironclad alibi.

Today was Sunday, but Jim couldn't go to church without possibly alerting the stalker that he and Crystal weren't together. So with time on his hands once again, Jim had turned his mind back to the book that was part of his cover story.

Unfortunately, he couldn't control the characters today any better than in the silent week before because his mind continually turned to the real mystery. The one he couldn't seem to solve or get out of his head. Plus the past had risen to haunt him, as well as the present and future.

"What am I supposed to be doing, Lord? Where am I supposed to be? And why won't You answer me?" he asked aloud, looking out the window at the distant sky. He closed his eyes but no answer came. God was being as elusive as Crystal's stalker. His eyes snapped open.

There it is again! I can't even pray without Crystal's stalker butting in.

Jim put his tea down and carefully repeated aloud his last thought. Slowly. Thoughtfully.

"I can't even pray without Crystal's stalker butting in."

He'd never had trouble praying from the very first day he'd accepted the Lord. Prayer had always been his refuge. But this wouldn't leave him alone.

And light dawned. He understood at last.

"That's it, isn't it, Lord? You've been answering me all along and I was too thick-headed to hear. That's why Crystal's problem keeps popping into my head. *You* sent me here. Because I'm a cop. Because I can help protect her."

It was like having the lights go on in a darkened room. Shadows took shape. Invisible objects suddenly appeared from nowhere.

Just because he'd almost been shot on that drug raid didn't mean he was in the wrong profession. His arm twinged again and he chuckled. Here he was on a leave of absence—a vacation, Crystal kept calling it—and he managed to get himself shot for the first time in his career. If he followed his previous logic, he'd have to give up free time. After all, the shootout at the bank had happened when he was off duty.

"I'm a cop!" he whispered, his voice surprising him with its reverent tone. "I'm *supposed* to be a cop. Yes!" he shouted as he stabbed his fist into the air and winced when his enthusiasm jarred his injured arm.

He looked back out the window and noticed a group of riders trot into the corral next to the barn where he'd learned to ride. Almost as one they dismounted and his stomached clenched.

Crystal was back.

Even from there he could see her inky braid swinging against her worn chambray shirt. She bounced down from the saddle and turned to speak to Tomas, then glanced toward the cabin. Jim couldn't make out her features, and he knew she couldn't see him standing there. Still, his body tightened with awareness. He had to find out who was threatening her. He had to find out why Jackson had left the way he had and why he was at Laurel Glen. And he had to do both soon.

Because Jim knew he had to get out of there before she became any more entrenched in his heart. It was a heart he'd built a wall around after Jessie's death. It was a wall she kept tunneling under, reaching him when he least expected it. A wall Crystal could easily undermine with proximity alone. He had to get out of there before that happened because he was never going to allow himself to love again—to risk feeling that kind of pain again.

He tried to move away from the window, but his feet felt nailed to the floor. So he told himself he'd just stay there and only watch her progress at her father's side toward the house. Trouble was, the longer he stood watching, the closer she got and the more he wanted to see her. Talk to her. Just talk. What harm could talking cause?

He'd missed her as much as he'd worried about her. And he wanted to tell her she'd been right about his career in law enforcement. He wanted her to know she'd helped him find his way.

Jim hated that she felt guilty over his injury. He wanted her to know his getting hurt was for the best since it had brought him to where he was now. His mind was clear about his place in the world and God's plan for him. He wanted her to know. He needed her to know. He was afraid he just plain needed her.

And that couldn't be. No. He just needed to talk to her. That was all! Jim reached up and rubbed his aching chest, telling himself it didn't matter that he was in this deep even though all they'd done so far was talk. Talking was safe. It had to be.

"Crystal!" he shouted as he stepped out onto the small stone porch of the log cabin. He had to laugh when she gasped. Crystal covered her heart with her hand and jumped back off the porch step, already on her way to see him.

"I heard great minds think alike," she quipped. "You look better."

"You don't look so bad yourself," Jim told her, and felt a surge of anger when he saw disbelief cross her features before she could look away. He wanted a chance to have a little heart-to-heart with every man who had ever contributed to the less-than-perfect image she had of herself. Every woman, too. Where was it written that beauty only came in small packages? To his way of thinking there was just more of Crystal to look at. To admire. To love.

Not that he did! No way. But her height and the size of her jeans had nothing to do with why not and everything to do with protecting himself from future pain. If that made him a coward, so be it. But he was not so cowardly that he'd skirt this issue with her. The least he could do before he left Colorado was help her see herself as she was and not as a brainwashed society did. Thin might be in, but beauty really was in the eye of the beholder, and as far as he was concerned, Crystal was a knockout.

"Ya know, I don't understand why you see yourself through such a distorted mirror." He paused, reflecting. "No. I take that back. These brain-dead bozos around here have you thinking you're less than you are because there's more to you than they're comfortable with. And do you know why? Because you intimidate them. You challenge their manhood just by walking into a room. To them, size and strength are what makes them superior. Of course, they're idiots who don't get that it's character that makes a man, so what can I say about them that I haven't?''

"It isn't just the men, Jim. Women feel the same way, only they make cutting remarks. The guys just treat me like one of them. I prefer that. Believe me.''

Now he really had a head of steam. "The women? Don't you have any idea why they treat you like...what was it you called yourself...an Amazon? I saw the looks at church when we walked in. And at Rusty's place the night we had dinner. Envy, pure and simple. They wish they had what you have. You walk into a room and stand out just because you are. You roll out of bed, looking a hundred times better than they do after hours in front of a mirror. So would you quit selling yourself short and go shower and change into something a little fancier? I want to take you out to dinner after evening services.''

She blinked, clearly bewildered. "Dinner?''

Jim fought the urge to roll his eyes. "You know, the meal you eat a few hours after lunch. Maybe as the sun's going down. Linguini in rosa sauce. Blackened salmon. Surf and turf. *Dinner.*''

"I'll just go get ready.'' She turned and walked down off the porch but stopped once on the walk, pivoting to face him again, her expression grave. "Is this...a date?''

Heaven help him, he couldn't deny it. But fear clogged his throat. He nodded and prayed she didn't read too much into his invitation. He didn't know if he could stand killing the hope that had suddenly come alive in her gaze.

Crystal tore up the steps and along the hall, nearly knocking her father over on his way out of his room. He was freshly showered and dressed in what she'd always thought of as his city clothes.

"Jim asked me to dinner after evening services so we won't be riding to church with you," she told him, unable to fight the smile pulling at her mouth. She had a real, would-you-have-dinner-with-me date!

Her father's eyebrows shot up. Though he said nothing, it was clear he was surprised that she had a date. Like all the other men, her father seemed to think she was only suited to date the Hulk.

"Hmm. I'm headed to Denver after church so that works out well. I have an early-morning meeting. I should be home sometime late tomorrow."

"That's better than driving all that way in the morning, I suppose." She reached out and put her hand on his forearm. "Dad, you look tired for such a long drive tonight. You aren't ill and keeping it from me, are you? You've been out of town an awful lot lately."

"There's nothing wrong with me," he all but growled, and pulled his arm away. "And since when am I subject to reporting my comings and goings to you?"

Crystal was no less shocked than if he'd struck her.

He never raised his voice to her. "Pardon me for my concern!"

He at least had the good grace to look shamefaced. "I'm sorry. I have a phone call to make," he muttered, and turned away.

Crystal stared after him, fighting foolish tears. Far from being reassured, she was more worried and hurt by his abrupt dismissal. He might ignore her, but he'd never taken a tone like that with her! It appeared their relationship could get worse. It just had.

Why did she keep trying? Why did she still care? Maybe she'd take a page out of her brother's book. Maybe she should try not caring, not trying or worrying about the father who had ignored them most of their lives. She was his daughter. Maybe she could get as good at ignoring him as he'd always been at ignoring her.

Squaring her shoulders, Crystal stalked into her room and pulled her favorite outfit from the closet, a blouse and matching pants made of a mauve microfiber. She'd found it in a dress shop in Greeley two years earlier.

The shop's owner had all but dragged her over to it when she and Julia had gone inside looking for work clothes suitable for a librarian. Crystal had protested that she wasn't the one shopping, but Julia had twisted her arm into trying on the outfit. As soon as Crystal got the pants and simple shirt on, she'd known why the woman said it was made for her. No one else would ever have bought it because both pieces actually fit her—a minor miracle! In flats, the only kind of dress shoes she ever wore, the pants were the perfect length.

About to head into the bathroom, she had to detour to answer the phone. It was Julia.

"Hello, stranger. Where on earth have you been? I've left numerous messages."

"Remember, I told you I had to help bring the cattle in closer to better water and grass?" Crystal asked.

"Oh, for heaven's sake, of course. Where's my head? So did the big blond hunk go along or stay behind to write?"

Crystal looked at the clock beside her bed. She didn't have time for a long heart-to-heart with Julia. "Listen, speaking of Jim, he's asked me to dinner after services tonight, and I just now got in from the roundup. I hate to rush you, but I've got to get in the shower."

"Dinner, as in a date?"

"Uh…actually, yes. A real date. Incredible, huh?"

"About time, I'd say! Wear that incredible outfit you got at the Carousel Shop in Greeley. That'll knock him dead!"

After those shots aimed at Jim rang out, *dead* was no longer a word she felt comfortable using carelessly. "Not if I don't wash up, I won't. Or maybe I will! I really have to run. Maybe we'll see you at church."

"Count on it."

Crystal hung up, took a fast shower, dried her hair rather than let it air dry as usual and she was ready. She looked herself in the mirror and shrugged nervously. This was as good as she got and Jim had seen her after two weeks of camping, washing in portable showers with trucked-in water. It had to be an improvement.

The Reverend Carson, their new young minister, preached an impassioned message but Crystal couldn't get her mind off Jim sitting close beside her long enough to find it even thought-provoking. They were headed out of church, the organist playing a tune she was too distracted to name, when someone tapped her on the shoulder. Crystal turned to find Julia's friendly smile beaming up at her. She and Julia exchanged hugs.

"You made it," Julia said as they stepped apart, her eyes straying to Jim.

"Julia, you remember Jim?"

"Yes, we met at the library just after you arrived," she said, giving Jim her hand when he held his out. "Then we met again the same week when you two giggled your way into my library."

Jim shook his head, drawing his hand back after giving Julia's fingers a gallant squeeze. "Never giggled in my life. Crystal was the giggle offender. I, on the other hand, was the picture of decorum."

"In your dreams," Crystal retorted. Julia meanwhile looked like a spectator at a tennis match.

"Well, after that, you both disappeared off the face of the earth to go play with dangerous cattle. I was surprised to hear you went along, Jim. I'd have thought you had more research to do for your book."

"I took the opportunity to learn how to play cowboy."

"Cowhand," Crystal corrected with a laugh.

"Oh, right. I have to get all the jargon straight if I'm ever going to get the first draft of the book done right."

Julia sobered. "I guess you aren't getting the time you planned to write. Did you stay with her out there to keep her safe?"

"That was the idea," Jim replied, his eyes scanning the remaining church members.

"Well, as Crystal's best friend, I thank you for that. I take it nothing's happened since you were nearly killed in your truck by this maniac?" Julia asked, looking at her. Crystal could still see the near panic she'd witnessed when Julia learned of the incident on the road from town. There was a touch of it in her eyes again now.

"He fired shots at me, but he missed by a mile," Jim lied smoothly.

Crystal was grateful that he must have seen Julia's anxiety. Remembering his hasty retreat to the stacks that day, she knew Jim didn't want a repeat of the scene in the library and she certainly didn't want Julia swooning in the sanctuary.

"Jim, please tell this stubborn woman to call her brother for help."

"I think I've been insulted," Jim teased.

Julia blushed scarlet. "Oh I didn't mean…"

Jim's quiet laughter rippled around them. "Relax, Julia. I took no offense. But I gather her brother has his reasons for not being here. And I can handle watching out for Crystal. It isn't much of a chore. Really.''

"You're very gallant, Jim, but you aren't getting any writing done. And sooner or later you'll have to leave. Maybe that's why he shot at you. Maybe he was trying to scare you off.''

"Well, if he was, he wasted his time," Jim said, and checked his watch. "I don't scare.''

Crystal checked hers as a reflex. "Oh, look at us going on and losing track of time! We have reservations in Greeley. I hate to rush off, Jule. But now that I'm back, we can have lunch on Wednesday. Okay?''

"Maybe this week we can pack our lunches and eat on the square," Julia suggested.

As if she hadn't had enough of eating outside in the past three weeks. But Julia rarely got out. "Good idea. But don't bother with your lunch. I'll get Anna to whip up something special for us.''

"That sounds wonderful. And if you talk to Jackson, give him my best.''

"I would, but I doubt I'll talk to him. Dad somehow managed to keep from spilling the beans about this stalker problem to him and I don't want to risk it, either. I don't want him to feel obligated to come home.''

"It's your life," Julia said, looking down at her hands and fumbling a bit with her purse. "Goodness," she said with an embarrassed chuckle in her voice, "I left the book I brought for Reverend Carson in the pew. Excuse me. I'd better get it now while I'm thinking about it.''

"Go. We have to hit the road anyway," Crystal told her, and they all went on their way.

"Well handled," she told Jim once in the parking lot. "I'll be forever grateful that you didn't tell her you were shot." She smiled at him as he held the door and handed her into the driver's seat of one of the Circle A's newer pickups. Jim's arm still wasn't up to handling a half-ton truck, no matter how upgraded the model, so she played chauffeur.

He got in and popped a CD in the player, then he chuckled. "I got a mental picture of Julia keeling over and figured God would forgive me for saving Him from having that scene in the library replay in His house."

"I'm certain you're right," she said deadpan. Then she lost control of the laughter that bubbled up.

Jim grinned back, shaking his head. "She sure has a lot of faith in your brother. What does she think he can do that I can't? I'm telling you, I'm starting to get a complex. Is this brother of yours a superhero?"

"I think you're seeing ancient history at work," she said putting the car in gear. "She's nothing if not loyal. Joe King didn't only torture me. He went after Julia, which was really pathetic, considering she was a little bit of a thing then, too. Her parents left her with her aunt and he'd tease her relentlessly, telling her that even her parents couldn't stand to look at her. After Jackson mopped up the playground with him, Joe left Julia alone, as well as me. She used to have a crush on Jackson. And she was pretty embarrassing about it in high school. It's a shame, too, because I think she's the kind of woman my brother needs.

Kind. Gentle. He's been hurt by every woman he's ever dated. Unfortunately, Jackson still isn't very comfortable around her because of how obvious she was about her feelings back then.''

"Oh."

She looked over. Jim was frowning, clearly confused.

"What?"

"I got the impression you three were like the three musketeers of Torrence."

"No. I don't really have much in common with Julia, though I do like her. She has no close friends but me. Her aunt had the chance to move in with her ailing sister, and Julia saw that it would be better for her, so she convinced her to go. Now she's all alone. It doesn't hurt me to have lunch with her once a week and occasionally go shopping and have dinner with her. I can't desert her. She needs me."

"So, she isn't your best friend at all."

Crystal's heart ached suddenly. Soon she'd be as alone as Julia. Because Julia was right. Jim couldn't stay forever. Especially now that his soul-searching had reaped the benefit of clarity in his life. He needed to return to his job. To God's plan for his life.

"No, I'm *her* best friend," she said, turning out onto the highway that led to Greeley. "Jackson's my best friend. Always has been and always will be, I guess."

Because pretty soon you'll be gone and you're the only one I've ever met who I feel closer to than my brother. You've made a special place for yourself in my heart. A place you'll probably never know about.

Chapter Fourteen

They made good time and were in Greeley in plenty of time for their reservations. La Casa Americana had a wonderful blend of Mexican and American entrées. She and Jackson often drove there for a night away from the ranch when one or both of them needed time away. But—after the blowup with her father, Crystal now wished she'd suggested somewhere else.

"Are you all right?" Jim asked after they were seated. There was concern in his expression, as well as his tone.

Crystal took a deep breath. "It's all getting to be a little much, I guess."

He reached across the table and took her hand, giving it a reassuring squeeze. Where usually his touch was exciting, this time, it nearly brought Crystal to tears.

"My father went off on another mysterious trip to Denver after church tonight. He said he had an appointment in the morning."

"Did you ask what was up? I know you've been concerned about all the trips into Denver."

A waiter appeared, so Jim let go of her hand and sat back. She thought it would give her time to collect herself, but instead she felt so bereft and alone that her distress mounted.

Crystal waited to answer until the waiter took their beverage and appetizer order and left. "I told him I was worried about him. I asked him if he was sick. He almost took my head off. I guess I found out what's worse than being ignored in favor of the Circle A. If I didn't love that ranch so much, I'd hate it."

Jim frowned. "He does seem awfully wrapped up in it. I have to agree there."

"It's everything to him."

"I don't understand that. It's wonderful. Don't get me wrong, but it's just a place. It'll pass away. His obsession doesn't fit with a man of faith."

"I guess you'd need to know where he came from. The ranch didn't start out to be my dad's. He lived in a series of foster homes as a kid. Ranchers and farmers took him on more as paid slave labor than as a child to nurture and care for. My grandmother used to tell us that because of that, he just didn't know how to show us how much he loved us.

"He met my mother when he showed up at the ranch looking for work. He was a runaway—only sixteen—but he lied about his age. Our grandfather hired him and taught him ranching, but he died before my parents were married. My grandmother and mother wanted Dad to feel like he was part of the ranch. For a wedding gift they renamed the ranch the Circle A.

A for Alton. The start of a new family. His family. My mother was seventeen, and he was nineteen by then.''

She sighed, thinking how happy they must have been together. Wishing she could find that kind of happiness. Maybe she was better off without it. Looking at Jim's handsome features across the table, grim with concern for her, her heart constricted. He'd be gone soon and she'd be alone—more alone than she'd been before his arrival. For the first time, Crystal could imagine the depth of her father's grief. But she never would have grieved the way her father had—to the detriment of his own children.

"Grandmother said Mama wanted to give him a family in the worst way. She tried for four years, then they decided to adopt when a church member was giving a baby up for adoption. That baby was Jackson. When I was born to them it was a great surprise. What they didn't know was that the difficulty she'd had getting pregnant was a precursor of ovarian cancer. Dad loved her to distraction and he's never gotten over her death. Since then, he's been obsessed with the Circle A. Making it thrive. Grow. He isn't building it for himself, but to keep what he sees as a sacred vow to her and my grandmother.''

"It must have been harder for your brother than you." When she tilted her head a bit and gave him a puzzled look, Jim explained his thinking. "Growing up being ignored and knowing he wasn't your father's biological son. He must have felt—'' he seemed to search for the right word "—unwelcome.''

Crystal fiddled with the basket of breadsticks. "Actually, my father never told him he was adopted. We learned later he was supposed to be told. Part of the adoption contract with the birth mother was that she'd wanted him to know of his heritage and how to find her. I don't think Jackson would ever have known, but last spring, he decided to move into the cabin where you're living. Mama had used it as a studio. She loved to paint. Dad kept it like a shrine all that time. Exactly as she left it.

"So we set to cleaning it out. One day Jackson came walking into the house, looking as if his whole world had been torn apart. It had been. He'd found his adoptions papers and a letter about his biological family."

Jim winced. "Wow. That's really tough. My family has always been the one big constant I can count on. That must have been a terrible blow. So he took off?"

"Not right away. He hung in there, trying to work things through with Dad. Dad wasn't a bad father. He just wasn't a very good one. We decorated the cabin, and Jackson moved in, but he couldn't forget that he had a biological family out there. Family that had wanted him to know who they were. He left in June hoping to meet some of them."

The waiter arrived with their salads. For a moment they both concentrated on eating, but Crystal couldn't shake the mood. Poor Jim deserved to know at least what had sparked it.

"Julia keeps reminding me that Jackson's gone by trying to get me to call him. She mentions him, and I remember that he hasn't even called to talk to me. I feel as if I've lost my brother—my best friend. And on top of that, I got stuck with Jackson's job. I don't want it. I hate dealing with the cattle and the sun and the men.

"And here's a shocker no one knows about." Her anger swelling, Crystal accidentally broke a breadstick she hadn't realized she had in her hand. "Before Jackson took off, I'd been planning on leaving. I have a degree in business. I minored in finance. I was offered a job at a bank in Greeley. I'd even found a place nearby to board Lady. I'm so sick of being the second son."

"He knows you aren't his son. Your father may have faults but he's not blind. I'm not sure, but I'd bet you've always been able to do whatever he's asked, right?"

Crystal had to concede that, yes, she was capable of doing the job of foreman. She just hated it.

"He may hand you jobs that are usually a man's, but I doubt he'd have come to me for help if there was someone stalking your brother."

Crystal could only shrug in answer. She didn't know what went on in her father's mind.

"My father was a rough-and-tumble cop who lived and breathed his kids," Jim said, "but he'd still throw a ball too hard to Joy every once in a while and she'd end up fighting tears. But she had a mother who'd see her bruised palm, for instance, and light into the old man like a mad hornet. Dad had Mom to constantly remind him that Joy was a girl—and he still forgot. Maybe you need to remind your father.

"The funniest night of our lives was the night Joy went to her senior prom. She came downstairs in this long clingy dress with tiny little straps holding it up. I swear, if Dad had had false teeth, they'd have dropped right out on the floor. Then in the blink of an eye, he was looking at her date like public enemy number one. Till then, Brian was someone Dad thought was just fine to be hanging around his daughter. How about your brother? He know he has a sister, not a brother?''

She nodded and smiled at the memory. ''When I was in my midteens, he dragged me to self-defense lessons. He thought he saw some of the men eyeing me with lust on their minds! He was worried one of them might not be trustworthy one day. He didn't need to worry, of course, but it was nice to know someone had noticed besides Grandmother that I was changing.''

Jim looked away as the waiter returned to take their entrée order. He ordered a steak dinner and Crystal ordered the same.

When she glanced back at Jim, he had an assessing look on his face. ''You didn't tell your brother about the job at the bank, did you?''

She shook her head. ''He'd have stayed. I didn't want to keep him here when he needed to be somewhere else. We did argue, though. I thought he was going about it all wrong. But Jackson's stubborn. I guess that's why he didn't say goodbye. We'd said it all. He just got up one morning, took his saddle and left for Pennsylvania.''

Jim choked on his ginger ale. *Not now,* a discordant voice in his brain screamed. *But this is why I'm here,* another shouted. He took a deep breath. *Right* then, he didn't want her venturing further down that path. He hated the idea of directly lying to her, but she was so upset and he didn't want to add to it with a confession that he was there on false pretenses.

"Sorry. That went down the wrong pipe," he said, after fully regaining his breath. He'd been trying to get her back on the subject of her life. Her dreams. He'd just have to try harder. "So he was gone and you fell into his position, but you still have to keep up your old work, too? No wonder you're worn-out."

"Dad and I sort of split both jobs, but there was more work than the three of us could do comfortably already. Jackson's working as a foreman at a horse farm in Pennsylvania. He applied as if he was a stranger, but he wasn't. He used friends as references as if the times he'd helped on their places had been jobs. That was one of the things I objected to. The other was not writing to his mother outright. My objection was *how* he planned to go, not the fact that he went."

Jim gave up trying to stop her from talking about her brother. Curiosity killed the cat, a voice in his head warned, but the prospect of solving the mystery he'd gone there to untangle tempted him. This didn't fit any of his or Cole's scenarios. He had to know.

"His mother?" Jim asked.

"She was the congregation member who placed Jackson with my parents. She was staying here with a distant relative while pregnant."

"Then what was her link to—"

"Laurel Glen," she said before he could say Pennsylvania.

He reacted too strongly to the name of the horse farm and she noticed.

"Is something wrong? Have you heard of Laurel Glen?"

Isn't half the truth better than none at all?

"Remember the story I told you about a farm owner's wife being killed by a horse while her son looked on? It happened at Laurel Glen."

"Jackson's mother is the sister of the current owner. She was engaged to Lieutenant Wade Jackson. Jackson was supposed to be named after him, but my parents turned the name around. My mother's grandfather was named Jack so I guess that's why."

"Ah, I wondered why everyone calls him Jackson and not Jack. Jackson gives him his own identity," Jim said, and almost added that they'd messed with the birth certificate later to get that name first.

"Some of his college friends call him Jack, but largely he gets the whole name. And, yes, it did give him his own identity. Until he learned he hadn't been named for an ancestor. He found out about the man he was really named for on the Internet. Wade Jackson was a chopper pilot in the Vietnam War. He was killed in the first week of his second tour of duty. Jackson's mother is Margaret Taggert, a Broadway actress who went by the name Meg. The Taggerts still own the farm. He's found her but, as far as I know, he's still keeping his identity a secret. I don't understand why, but Dad said he'd gotten off the phone rather abruptly because someone came into his office so it must still be a secret."

Oh, it's a secret, all right. Now I have to decide if I call and let the cat out of the bag.

Chapter Fifteen

Jim tossed down some bills and flipped the check holder closed. "Ready?" he asked, and Crystal nodded, a relaxed smile on her face.

Crystal's sprits had risen as she regaled him with stories of her brother and their childhood. The guy sounded like a prince among men, and someone Jim would have gotten along well with under different circumstances. It seemed as if once the floodgates had opened and she'd begun to talk about Jackson, she couldn't talk about anything else. But then Jim realized that she was part of every story she told, or her grandmother was. Brother and sister must have been inseparable. The way Tom Peterson and later, Greg were with him. One or both were in most of his boyhood and adolescent stories, as well. So he told her several of those tales about his own escapades on the basketball courts, baseball diamonds and playgrounds of Riverside.

Jim returned Crystal's infectious smile and stood

as she did. One thing he'd learned over the past month since meeting her was that he liked putting a smile on her face and drawing her ready laughter. Maybe because there was so little to smile about in her life right then.

And maybe because he just plain liked her.

He put a hand on her back at her waist and, for the first time, she didn't jump out of her skin as he moved her in front of him toward the exit. If he managed to leave her with a new sense of herself as a woman, he would be satisfied that he'd done something to make up for his lies of omission. But before he could leave her at all, he had to find out who was threatening her.

For the entire drive back to the Circle A, his senses tortured him, just as they had on the way to the restaurant. Crystal wore a light scent that he couldn't place, though it was familiar. But the name didn't matter. He knew that whatever it was, it drew him like a moth to a flame.

And if he wasn't really careful, both of them would get burned.

She didn't drop him off at the cabin, but parked in the area behind the main house. There, he was at least able to walk her to her door. He'd tried all evening to let her know that tonight, while not about happily-ever-after, was not about being *pals*. She opened her front door then turned back. And Jim felt careful planning, moderation and caution fly right out the proverbial window.

The moon hung in the sky at his back and in its silvery light she was breathtaking. Her hair shone as if sprinkled with diamonds, and it drew his fingers to its gleaming strands. He swallowed. Just as he'd thought—silk.

Her wide, slightly almond-shaped eyes twinkled like a deep water lake under a full moon as she stared at him. He caressed her cheek with his other hand and the rose-velvet texture dragged his thoughts, his gaze, to her lips. He had to feel them to see if they were as soft as they looked and to taste them to see if they were as sweet and tempting as he'd been imagining.

Their lips met as he cupped her head in his palms and he learned the awful, wonderful truth. He hadn't known what temptation was until he'd kissed Crystal Alton. She melted against him and he reveled in the feel of her solid strength as he pulled her close.

This was beyond anything Jim had ever thought possible. He felt her need. He knew her expectations. She didn't know he would never—could never—return the feelings she'd just betrayed. Just poured into him.

He feared her heartbreak. And his. This was more than helping her see other possibilities. This was surrender. Again—hers and his.

He could not—would not—risk the killing pain of watching her die someday. Soon, if he didn't find the man stalking her.

With immense effort, he skimmed his hands to her arms and set her away. There was a fiery light now in her exotic eyes and her lips were swollen from his kiss. "Go inside," he ordered. "Tomorrow we have to talk."

She backed inside, a shy smile tipping her perfect lips. Her eyes, dazed and unfocused, never left his face. And he knew he'd put that look on her face. It made him feel good. It made him feel terrible.

"Night," she whispered in a husky voice he'd hear in his dreams.

And in his nightmares.

"Night," he said, shocked that same rough tenor was in his own voice.

Jim waited to hear the lock slide into place before walking toward the cabin. He was in big trouble here. And Crystal, though not the least of it, was the most fragile. He hadn't meant to kiss her.

Hadn't meant to care.

Most of all, he hadn't meant that she should care for him. He was just supposed to be a ship passing in the night. A ship that woke her up. That showed her the way to another, more fulfilling life.

And then there was the other problem. The question of what to do with the revelations the night had brought to light. He'd gone to Colorado having made a promise. Trying to repay a debt. He didn't break promises and always paid his debts.

He hadn't quizzed Crystal. She'd volunteered the information about her brother. He'd even made an attempt, however short-lived, to direct the conversation another way. Talking about her brother had helped lift Crystal from despair. He'd been able to reassure her that Jackson wouldn't think of her as no longer family.

She hadn't asked him to hold her revelations in confidence. Most important, since Jackson wasn't at Laurel Glen for nefarious purposes, Jim's reporting the truth to Cole should hurt no one. Also, Jackson's sparse communication with home should make it safe for Jim to stay on.

Decision made, he moved into the cabin and sat down in the big chair facing the fireplace and dialed Cole on his cell phone.

Crystal all but floated into the house and flopped in the big comfy chair in her bedroom. She dropped her purse on the table next to her. And paper crinkled within. Odd, she hadn't put any paper in her purse. Maybe she'd stuck the church bulletin in. No. She'd been so distracted by Jim's presence and their late-evening dinner that she hadn't taken one.

A wave of trepidation washed over her as she reached for the little crocheted bag. Biting her lip, she dragged the paper into the light without even having to untie the bow that held the sides together in the middle.

"You were with him. Wearing your special mauve pants and top for him and not me. You smiled for him but you sneer at me. If I hadn't missed last week, he'd be dead and I'd have been with you. I've waited for you but now you've chosen him over me. Death over me. When you die you'll be thinking of me. Soon."

Crystal sucked a gulp of air. "Oh, Lord." She meant it as a prayer, but further words failed her. She took comfort in knowing God understood the fear in her heart.

Crystal blinked and knew what she had to do. She had to tell Jim. So she ran through the house and out the side door nearest the cabin. The front door stood open when she got there and through the screen door she could hear Jim talking to someone on the phone. And the world stopped spinning.

"…wanted you to know so you can relax, not go off the deep end. The man's record is squeaky clean. So now you know Jackson Alton is your cousin. We're square. Right?

"Good. I'll touch base when I get back. No. I have some loose ends to tie up here. Talk to ya."

Crystal stood frozen in the doorway as Jim stood and looked her way. He, too, froze.

She'd been a fool. She wasn't special. She wasn't desirable. Not to him. Not to anyone but a man bent on killing her. Attractive to a nutcase. She'd have laughed if she weren't fighting tears already. She was just the big gawky ranch rat she'd always been.

"Crystal, I—"

His voice broke her from her frozen mold. Not her heart. Just her faculties. "You used me," she accused, teeth gritted. She was surprised her voice sounded so clear. So direct. So unbroken with the tears raging on the inside.

"I didn't ask about your brother." So cool. He just stood there, his face expressionless.

"But you listened. You pretended to be my friend. Tell me. Is there a book? A career crisis? Is there even a stalker? Or was all this horror manufactured to make me need you?"

"Crystal, no. I didn't even know you existed when I came here, and you were getting threats long before I ever heard the name Jackson Alton. And anything I told you about me was the God-honest truth. Your brother told no one at Laurel Glen anything about himself. There was nothing I could learn long-distance so I had to come here to learn the truth. I owed Cole Taggert. Big-time.''

''Well, you paid big-time. You had to befriend me in order to pump me for information. Romance me. The kiss, though, was way over the top. You'd already learned all you came here for. You really shouldn't have thrown in the kiss. Definitely over-kill.''

''I did want to help. I do. What I did to keep you safe had nothing to do with why I came here.''

''How lovely. I, however, no longer want your help. Pack and be out of here in the morning. I never want to see your face again. Now that Caleb cleared Joe King, I have two law-enforcement officers to rely on. One of them may be an idiot, but at least I know he isn't trying to kill me. And don't try appealing to my father. He won't be any more forgiving than I am. Goodbye, Lieutenant Lovell. It's been an experience.''

Crystal could feel the ice melting. She wouldn't cry in front of this man! Without another word, she turned and stalked out. All the while, as she prayed for strength, she also prayed he'd call her back. Offer a good explanation. Declare his undying love. Then, when the only sounds that broke the silence were the songs of tree frogs and crickets, she prayed her love for him would die a fast death.

She reached the house and momentarily balked at entering. But this was her home. The man out there who was torturing her wasn't going to take that away. She went inside and locked the door.

At the foot of the stairs, Crystal stopped by the phone. Her hand was in place to lift the receiver and call the sheriff's department, but she realized she could easily get Joe King instead of Caleb. And she just wasn't up to that. And if she called Caleb directly, he'd tell Jim. And that she wouldn't have.

Nothing would happen that night, she told herself. She was safe at home. She'd call in the morning. Once Jim was gone.

Decision made, she kept the house in darkness, proceeding through the familiar space on instinct. The house at that moment seemed symbolic of her life within it. Isolated. Dark. Lonely. Once in her room, Crystal grabbed a tissue box off the bureau and fell on the bed.

She hated sleeping on a soggy pillow.

Jim stood watching as Crystal stalked out, then he followed her to the door. He didn't intend to stop her however much he wanted to. He just watched her flee into the house, then he stepped onto the porch and sank into a chair. He hadn't defended himself and he wouldn't.

Couldn't.

He'd seen the way she'd looked at him just minutes earlier when he'd kissed her good-night. There had been love in her eyes. He knew. That look had lived in the eyes of another—once upon a time. And when those eyes had closed forever, they'd taken his heart with them and left him as cold and empty as the shell he'd helped bury that rainy day at Riverside Memorial Park.

He had nothing to offer Crystal but more pain and heartache. Because even if he'd managed to explain away the lies of omission he was guilty of, he couldn't chance her thinking it changed anything. She'd already waited a lifetime for a love she was entitled to, but one he could not give her. He couldn't let her wait for his love, as well. Especially since he knew it would be a hopeless exercise.

No, better she think him a complete scum and liar. It was over, ended however painfully. But ended with a clean break.

Evan Alton turned onto the road leading to the Circle A. It was well past two in the morning, but he'd had to return home that night. Staying in Denver just hadn't been an option.

He couldn't believe he'd snapped at Cris the way he had because she'd become concerned for him. And he didn't need to talk to Dr. Campbell in the morning to know why he'd done it or why he'd known sleep would elude him if he didn't see his daughter and explain.

Guilt.

It weighed him down like a millstone.

That and grief. A load of both.

At the gateway to the Circle A drive, he stopped and looked up. Hanging there was the gift that had begun his emotional decline. Meant as a symbol of welcome and trust, it had been that for eight years. Then on a sunny day in May, when Martha had smiled at him and closed her eyes for the last time, it had become an icon of obsession and burden.

He'd lost Martha but she'd given him the Circle A and he'd been determined to see it thrive. To the exclusion of all else. Including the two most precious gifts she'd left in his care. Jackson and Cris. It was a sad commentary that only now, once he'd lost his son and now that Cris's life was threatened, had he woken up and seen what he'd done. Seen the damage he'd caused. Worse, there was probably more hurt than he could imagine bottled up inside the two best children a man could have.

And it was all his fault.

Shaking his head at the depth of his stupidity, Evan put the pickup in gear. He had to talk this out with Cris even if he had to wake her. It was way past time. As he passed the house and there were no lights on, he knew he'd have to wake her.

Years of long residence in the house made him comfortable moving through it in near pitch darkness. And it was only those years that had him pausing halfway through. There was an odor in the air he didn't equate with home. He sniffed deeply and coughed.

Propane!

Chapter Sixteen

He looked toward the stairs. Cris! Heedless, he ran then, tripping once in his haste, knowing the danger. The volatility. He had to get her out of there. Her door was thankfully closed, and she was asleep in her bed. The gas wouldn't have gotten to her yet.

"Cris," he said, rushing in.

"Daddy?" she asked, sobbing.

Something was wrong. He'd thought her closed door would have kept the gas from her. As he moved toward her by the light of the moon, Evan saw her sit up and reach for the light. He scrambled forward to grab her arm just in time. "Don't! You'll blow up the house and us with it."

"What?" She sniffled.

He let go of her and opened the window next to her bed. He did it slowly so the metal runners wouldn't create even the tiniest spark. "Cris, snap out of it!" he shouted, regretting the harshness of his tone but with no time to explain. What if it reached a pilot light? "We have to get out of here and there's no way I can carry you." He took her arm again. "Get up and move. The whole house is full of propane."

That seemed to do the trick. Snapped her wide-awake. Had her moving. She rolled to her feet and rushed with him toward the hall, along the balcony that stood over the entranceway and living room and dining area. The gas had so completely filled the house that both of them were gasping for breath by the time they were down the stairs. The nearest fresh air was the door at the side of the house across from the cabin.

Evan figured all their coughing and gasping was what brought Jim Lovell running. He had raced out of the cabin, wearing only jeans, his hair ruffled. "What happened?" he demanded.

"Gas," Evan gasped.

Lovell reached for Cris, concern for Evan's daughter written on his face even in the silvery light of a partial moon. Cris yanked her arm away and sat on the wall at the edge of the patio, surprising Evan.

"Right," Lovell said with a sigh. "I'll go see if I can find the source, sir. Cooking, hot water and heat?" he checked, and Evan could only nod that yes those were the uses for propane in the house. "I'll get some windows open and check for leaks. Don't worry."

He turned and was gone before Evan fully got his breath. "I should go back in and help," he said when he could talk. But Cris reached out for him, stopping him, though she couldn't touch him from that distance. Compelled to offer some sort of comfort, he went and sat next to her. He desperately wanted to find a way to bridge the gap between them.

"What are you doing here?" she asked him.

He looked at his daughter, silhouetted in the moonlight. She was so beautiful, it hurt to look at her. She was so much like Martha. "I couldn't sleep. I'm sorry I snapped at you. I appreciate your concern but it's unnecessary. Mind telling me what happened to the happy couple I left at church? That must have been one disappointing dinner."

She pulled a face. "It was the postdinner that was disappointing."

Evan felt outrage bloom. Had the man— "I shouldn't have left you alone here with him!"

"Oh, please, Dad," she said with an overabundance of what sounded to Evan like disbelief. "The man was forcing himself to be in my company. Why would he try to take advantage of me? He was here to investigate Jackson for the Taggert family. You just played into his hand by throwing us together."

"I wanted to know you were protected while I concentrated on business. I certainly didn't mean that you be hurt." Tentatively he put his arm around his daughter.

"I'm angry, not hurt," she hurried to correct. Hurried too much to be wholly believed.

"Then why the anger? I'd say he got the difficult end of the deal. He's the one who was shot while looking out for you."

Her chuckle held a bitter edge. "Oh, Dad, I doubt he realized your request to watch my back was as dangerous as it turned out to be. Big-city boy comes to the country. How dangerous could a bunch of hicks be?''

Jim's husky voice intruded. ''I found you scrambling in the dirt out on the access road after you were very nearly killed in a car wreck. I knew what trying to help you required from the start. And I sure knew how dangerous this guy was,'' Jim Lovell growled, joining them.

Evan hadn't heard a sound of his approach. Lovell moved like a cat no matter what his size. He held up his hand silently, asking the time to explain. Since the man had been shot on his land more or less in the service of his daughter, Evan saw no harm in granting that small courtesy. But Cris came back at Lovell, her voice tight with anger.

''I was not scrambling in the dirt. I was about to steal your truck! And I almost got to it. If I hadn't been hurt, you'd never have caught me!''

''I didn't come here to cause any of you trouble.'' Lovell ignored Cris and went on with his explanation. ''I moved with caution, yes. But I didn't have to. I did it this way so I wouldn't chance damaging your son's reputation if your neighbors learned he was being investigated by a police officer. I came here with an obligation to the Taggert family. They've had an unbelievably rough year, and I couldn't let them down. On my way here, I got a call that Ross Taggert—he's Laurel Glen's owner—suffered a stroke thanks to all the stress he's been under. His son was only trying to protect his father and his family when he asked my help.''

''Protect them from my son? My son is about the

least threatening person I've ever met, Lovell. Do they check all their employees this carefully?'' Evan demanded as Cris refused to even look toward the man. She was one hurt and angry woman.

"Of course they don't. You couldn't know this. And I doubt Jackson did before going to Laurel Glen. He doesn't just look like a possible branch off their family tree, he looks exactly like the main trunk. But he showed up and acted as if it was coincidence. It was too *much* coincidence for Cole to discount. And frankly for me, too.''

Evan couldn't say he'd have done differently. And Jim Lovell could have flashed that badge, questioned indiscriminately and caused the kind of damage he'd tried to avoid. "Ah. I begin to understand. Thank you for your caution, in that case, Jim.''

Cris finally spoke. "Thank him for his caution? Oh, that's rich!''

"So tell me what you found inside,'' Evan asked smoothly, hoping if he ignored Cris's remark, she too would see that he'd been right—for Jackson's sake anyway. Unfortunately, Jim Lovell had made a huge mistake on his daughter's part. Had he asked forthrightly and explained the worry at Laurel Glen, she would have told him all the same things and called Jackson.

Crystal looked on in amazement from her seat against the wall. What was this? A good old boys' club? Angry and flustered by Jim's presence while she paraded around in an old football jersey of her brother's, she couldn't keep from tuning in to what he said.

"The pilots were all blown out so I'd say this wasn't accidental. It's odd there was no note this time. He's moved off pattern again."

"No. I got a note," she admitted. Until it was safe to use a phone without threat of setting off a spark, he was the only police presence they had. "It's in my room on the dresser just inside the door. I'll go get it."

"Stay here. I can do it. I'll grab you a robe while I'm at it." Jim strode off and Crystal stood and confronted her father, hurt and anger in every inch of her body.

"How could you forgive him so readily?" she said.

Her father's eyebrows climbed higher. "You said he hadn't hurt you, just angered you."

"He investigated your son. He called this Cole Taggert and made a report on Jackson. There's no telling what fall out it will cause him."

"If Taggert throws him off his land, maybe your brother will wake up and come back here where he's needed."

"How can you wish that for him? Did it ever occur to you that he's looking for something there? Something he needs to find? Do you ever think of anyone but yourself?"

"I didn't tell him about this stalker when I knew it was the perfect way to get him home, did I? And I thought of you tonight. If I hadn't, you'd have been blown sky-high along with your mother's house."

But it still mutated into something about his precious Circle A, didn't it? She looked up as Jim came out the back door and around the corner toward them.

He'd apparently run down to get his big lantern/flashlight and in its glow she saw that he'd bagged the letter the way he had that night on the road. Just last month. A lifetime ago.

"The phone lines were cut, too. And it appears there *was* a warning. A strong one. Why on earth didn't you tell me?" he demanded.

He'd done a lot of demanding since arriving minutes ago. She faced him, crossing her arms. She wouldn't sit there and gaze up at him like some weak-kneed ninny. "I'd just learned you were nothing but a spy. Why on earth would I call on someone I don't trust for help?" she demanded in as cool a voice as he'd used earlier when reacting to her angry charges.

Jim ignored her barb and asked, "Did you smell the gas at all the two times you entered the house earlier tonight?"

Deciding too much protest would tell its own secret—the one that said she was reacting out of pain not anger—she thought about his question. "No. And I don't think I would have missed that."

"Okay," he said thoughtfully. "As I said, the pilots on all three appliances were blown out. When we came home earlier, you had to unlock the door to get in. You didn't lock the side door when you came over to the cabin a few minutes later? Did you have to unlock it to get out?"

"Yes, but how do you know I didn't lock it behind me?"

"Because I made sure you got inside okay. I heard you two bursting out of the house because I heard Evan's car and got up and walked down to the parking area to make sure it was someone who belonged here.''

Her father chuckled. "I didn't even hear you. Where are you going with this, Lovell?"

"I think he was in the house with Crystal. There's no forced entry. He had to have gone in when Crystal came out to the cabin, but he couldn't have gotten all three blown out and the phone lines cut in that short time. He had to have been in there with her."

Crystal sank back to the stone wall again. He'd been that close. He could have come into her room and done his worst while she lay crying and masking his movements. She shuddered, not knowing how much more she could take.

"I'm going to run over and use my cell to call this in to Caleb or King. Let's hope it's Caleb who's on tonight."

Fifteen minutes later they got King. A very different Sheriff King. An extremely apologetic King. He'd botched possibly the only important case that would ever come his way and it had become big news locally. And he'd annoyed one of the most important men in town.

"First, I'd like to apologize, Cris, Evan. I misjudged this whole thing. It grieves me that I was so far off, I became a suspect. We may never be friends with so much water under the bridge, but I wouldn't want anything to happen to you, your friends or family. I'm truly sorry."

The man did look as if he regretted the way he'd acted. He shifted from foot to foot and hung his head sheepishly.

"Forget it, King," Jim said, stepping out of the shadows. "They aren't going to vote for you come November if you kowtow to them on the town square."

Crystal had to bite her lip to keep from laughing, but then she realized how presumptuous Jim was being. He'd given up any right to make statements as if he spoke for her. So, hard as it was, she walked over to the paunchy sheriff and put her hand out. "No hard feelings, Joe. Just find this guy before he kills someone."

"Well, now, that isn't going to be all that easy. I think Jim will bear me out on this. We got nothing, Cris. Unless that car rolls into one of the body shops Lovell alerted or the APB bears fruit. This guy's mighty clever. Ain't that right, Lovell?"

"This might have prints on it," Jim said, handing him the latest threat. "Or not. The last one didn't."

"That's my point. I called Hart on my way over here and he agrees. We think you ought to go off somewhere. Give Caleb and me time to flush this guy out. Start finding out who in a fifty-mile radius even owns a car fitting those paint samples. It's all we could come up with to do what we haven't done. I wouldn't guess that would be practical near where Lovell hails from. But here, though it'll be a big job, it is possible."

"I haven't been anywhere farther than Denver in my entire life. Where would I go?"

"Visit your brother," Jim suggested.

"He'll be out of a job come morning with no place to stay, thanks to you!"

Jim didn't blink. He just shook his head. "You don't know the Taggerts. That isn't going to happen. I nearly put Cole in prison by mistake and they don't shoot me on sight. Cole was just worried. He said his father was thrilled with your brother's work."

"I'll give him a call in the morning. It's a good idea, Cris," her father said, joining the conspiracy. "Jim, you can trade your rental in at the airport in Denver. I'll pay for your ticket and you can escort her to Philadelphia."

As Jim was nodding, she was declaring, "No way am I going anywhere with him!"

"He can't drive yet. He has to fly and you shouldn't go alone." Her father said it so reasonably she wanted to scream.

"How he gets home isn't my problem. I'll just stay here and he won't need to keep me safe."

"You have to go. You can't stay here. It's too dangerous. The whole house could have gone up tonight."

Crystal stepped back, and for the second time in less than a day, felt as if he'd struck her. She stared at her father. He wanted her gone.

She'd suspected the truth, of course. Grumbled and groused to Jackson in the throes of teenage angst that it was the truth. But now she knew for sure, and it was worse than she, in her heart of hearts, had ever fully accepted until now. Not just the ranch as a business, but even the house by itself was more important to her father than she was.

Chapter Seventeen

Jim stood outside of Philly International's D terminal waiting for Greg Peterson to pick him up. It was one of those rare summer days in southeastern Pennsylvania when a Canadian cold front swept in, bringing sixty-degree weather and cool breezes. But the beauty of the day and the vague feeling of homecoming couldn't erase the pain of watching Crystal where she stood farther down the sidewalk waiting for her own ride.

She'd refused to walk with him to their gate at the Denver airport. Then she'd requested her seat on the plane be changed. To anywhere but next to his. And when he'd tried to walk with her to the baggage claim area after debarking, she ordered him to stay away from her.

As he watched, a teal extended-cab pickup pulled up and Crystal smiled genuinely for the first time since last night. He missed her so much already. His heart aching and full of impotent regret, Jim saw

Jackson Alton leap out of the pickup, scoot around the hood and scoop Crystal into his arms in an affectionate bear hug.

Then, smiling broadly, the man he'd gone to Colorado to investigate, turned and put his arm gently around a tall willowy blonde who'd climbed down out of the pickup. He was introducing her to Crystal when Jim recognized the blonde. Her name was Elizabeth Boyer and she and Cole Taggert had been an item during his investigation at Laurel Glen. He'd thought they still were, but seeing the open affection between her and Alton, Jim thought there was a good chance that status had changed. Crystal all but leaped out of her boots as Alton spoke, then she suddenly hugged Elizabeth. They all looked so happy, as if some sort of celebration were in order.

Jim worried for the first time that Cole might have had an ulterior motive for wanting Jackson Alton investigated.

"Earth to Lovell," he heard his oldest friend say.

He shook Greg's hand. "I didn't see you arrive," Jim admitted as his eyes strayed back down the walkway.

"My point exactly. Aren't vacations supposed to be about rest? What's with the circles under the eyes and sling on the arm?"

"Short or long story?" Jim asked, unable to take his eyes off Crystal. She'd been angry at him but otherwise she seemed okay—certainly happy to be with her brother and to meet Elizabeth Boyer.

Maybe he hadn't hurt her, after all, Jim decided. He sent a quick prayer upward, wishing she'd cared enough to be hurt then quickly thanking God that she hadn't. He wanted only good things for Crystal.

"I'll take the short version for now," Greg responded.

"I tried to help somebody and got shot. It's the reason I needed the lift home. You're sure you have the time for this today?"

"It's fine. It'll give me the chance to stop in on Jim Dillon sans the Peterson herd. He's meeting me in his office at the Tabernacle. He's your pastor now. You want to come along?"

Jim thought for a minute then shook his head. He wasn't ready to talk about what he was feeling.

Greg gestured toward the Alton reunion at the end of the terminal's walkway. "Does the blonde have a part in the longer version?"

Again Jim shook his head, drinking in one last look at Crystal. "The taller one with the long black hair," he answered absently.

"It's nice to see your taste is still way above average even after years of self-imposed exile from women."

Jim shot Greg an annoyed frown. "I have women friends. Does Angelica know you're out window-shopping while she's carrying your third child?"

Greg grinned. "I'm not dead. I'm married. A condition that brings me a lot of happiness and one I happen to covet for my best friend."

Shaking his head, attention still drawn to Crystal, he growled. "It'll never happen."

"Because your warrior princess is crawling into

some other guy's pickup? Or is that why she's not with you?''

Warrior princess? He sighed. Yeah. It fit. ''Same long story,'' Jim said. Knowing he wouldn't avoid telling the whole sorry tale before the drive to his apartment was over, he sighed. ''Come on. Let's get me loaded up and I'll fill you in on one really complicated freebie undercover assignment.''

Jim bent to pick up his laptop. As he straightened, the teal pickup drove by. His gaze connected with Crystal's for a split second and a sense of loss so profound, it nearly took him to his knees, swept over him.

He loved her.

Hadn't he promised himself not to do this again? Yeah, he had, but this pain sure felt like lost love to him. And he should know.

He'd felt it before.

Crystal knew she should be fascinated by the view of Philadelphia's tall buildings in the distance. She was, but when her gaze had connected with Jim's, the pain of knowing she'd never see him again pounced from behind the shadow of her anger and tore at her heart.

''Talk,'' Jackson ordered from the driver's seat as he steered onto an entrance ramp marked I-95 South.

''Don't we go through the city?'' she asked, looking back at the tall buildings in the distance silhouetted against the clear blue sky. ''I was hoping we would. It seems a shame to be near one of the largest cities in the country and not get to see it up close. Although it does look lovely at a distance—''

''If I'd wanted idle chatter,'' Jackson interrupted, ''I would have put on local talk radio. But then again it isn't anywhere near as mindless as all that nonsense you were just spouting. What happened at home last night besides our father treating you like a liability? You said you'd tell me once you got here. So spill it.''

Crystal blew out a breath. There was no fooling her brother. They knew each other too well. ''It started around mid-August. Dad rented out the cabin to a wolf in sheep's clothing, named Jim Lovell.''

''Cole's cop,'' Jackson said.

She nodded. ''He pretended to be my friend. Pretended to care about me. He took me on a date last night. Kissed me good-night. But during dinner I'd confided in him about you and why you left. The first thing he did was call Cole Taggert to tell him who you are to his family. I overheard the call when I went to tell him about the latest threatening note I got. I hope it didn't cause you trouble—me telling him about you. I'm so angry...and...and...''

''Hurt,'' Elizabeth said, naming the emotion Crystal hated admitting to.

''I was such an idiot. He kept telling me things...'' She sniffled, tears burning at the back of her throat, filling her eyes. ''Things I wanted to hear. He said all the guys in Torrence were idiots for not asking me out. For treating me like a pal. He said I was his ideal woman. I actually thought he cared about me. *Me.*

The local Amazon! But he'd been lying to me the whole time.''

Jackson's brand-new fiancée turned in her seat, her eyes full of sympathy. ''I know the feeling,'' she said, a slightly annoyed edge to her voice as she glanced pointedly at Jackson.

And Jackson blushed like a schoolboy.

''You didn't know why my brother was at Laurel Glen, either?'' Crystal asked Elizabeth.

''Not till this morning I didn't.''

Crystal smacked him lightly on the back of the shoulder.

''Hey, no hitting the driver. I was under obligation to my mother to keep her secret until she was ready,'' Jackson defended. ''My birth was her secret to reveal to her family and I'd promised not to say anything. I know how those kinds of restrictions feel or Lieutenant Lovell and I would have had a little talk back there. I still might have a few things to say to him now that I know he messed with your feelings.''

''Don't you dare. He doesn't have a clue how I feel and I don't want him to know. I'd be mortified if he found out.''

''But—''

''I mean it, Jackson Wade Alton!''

''Jack, listen to your sister,'' Elizabeth said quietly.

And for what surely was the first time in his life, her stubborn brother gave up without an argument. He simply nodded, and in what *was* Jackson's style, shot Beth a teasing grin and said, ''Yes, dear,'' in a twangy nasal whine.

Elizabeth laughed and Crystal sat back. Jim was a

lot like her brother—her best friend. A tease with a serious protective side. It was no wonder they'd gotten along so well. Except that the feelings he'd elicited in her were anything but brotherly.

Oh, what was the use in letting her mind stray there? Jim was history. Maybe someday she'd be able to take out the memories of the roundup and their long conversations around a campfire, and look upon them if not fondly, then at least as a learning experience.

"So tell me, you two. When's the wedding?"

Crystal walked into the stable, wiping the sweat off her forehead. It had been a week since her arrival in Pennsylvania and the changeability of the weather there amazed her. Since she'd arrived, it had gone from a cool clear eighty to a damp sixty-five before the thermostat had begun to climb. It was now a hot, muggy ninety and it was only ten in the morning.

Laurel Glen was as different from the Circle A as Pennsylvania weather was from Colorado's. The farm as a whole reminded her of something out of an old forties movie. The Taggerts actually dressed for dinner! All that was missing was Ginger Rogers and Fred Astaire waltzing on Laurel House's stone terraces.

The operation was impressive. The farm consisted of four long brick stable buildings, a tall octagon-shaped barn, verdant pastures of freshly mowed grass. It sat nestled among green, rolling hills. And lining those hills were miles of bright white board fencing that stretched beyond the horizon.

As she made her way to Jackson's office, a beautiful Morgan Horse stuck her head out and whinnied. The brass plaque on the stall door read Queen Morgana. Crystal couldn't ignore the animal's demand for attention. After making friends with the dark horse, she turned away and walked toward her brother's office.

"Hey, sis. Got a letter here for you," he said when she stuck her head in to make sure he wasn't busy. He seemed so at home there at Laurel Glen that she actually began to think her father might have lost him after all. She smiled knowing she, at least, hadn't. He might not wind up in her day-to-day life now, but he'd always be there for her when she really needed him.

Crystal took the envelope he held out. Puzzled, she stared at the handwriting. She'd thought it might have been from Julia, but the penmanship was completely foreign to her. And it wasn't mailed from Torrence but from Loveland. Her legs felt a little shaky and she sank into the chair across from Jackson's desk. No one but Caleb, Sheriff King, their father and Jule knew where she was.

She tore it open. "I can't imagine who'd—" The rest of the thought stuttered in her brain. All she could do was stare at the ugly words pasted on the page.

You thought you could run away? Didn't you know my heart would find you? It has and now I'm coming there to find my love. Enjoy these days. They'll be your last.

Jackson's voice calling her name penetrated the fear-invoked fog in her brain. He was kneeling on the floor in front of her, peeling her fingers apart to take the letter. "No. Put it in a plastic bag. Th-there might be fingerprints on it. That's what Jim always did."

"Okay. And speaking of *Jim,* I think we'll just take this to him."

"No. I don't want to see him. Call the police."

"He *is* the police around here. This area of the county doesn't have its own police force. The state police handles our problems."

"Oh. Then I want another cop."

"Honey, Jim Lovell may be the lowest man you've ever met, but he is a good police officer, and right now we need that. Plus, he has knowledge of this guy. He's been working on this for weeks. Now come on. We're going to take a ride."

"But—" She looked at him and knew by the stubborn set of his jaw that she'd already lost the argument. "Poor Elizabeth. Does she know how often you get your own way?"

Jackson grinned. "Don't go feeling sorry for her. She's worse than me."

"Right! And I believe in little green men! Why don't you go without me and take the letter? You know as much about it as I do."

Jackson's grin widened and took on a lethal edge. "You really want to put me by myself in a room with the man who broke my little sister's heart."

Crystal stood. "That was blackmail!" she accused.

"Whatever works," he quipped, and steered her out the door.

Chapter Eighteen

"We need to speak to Lieutenant Lovell," Jim heard some guy in the hall say. Probably another department shrink.

"Room twenty-two. Three doors down," the annoyingly cheerful voice of Cary Stephens, his sometimes partner, said. "I'd knock, though. He's been in a real mood since he came back."

"I heard that," Jim yelled loud enough to be heard in the hall.

"Well, if this don't cheer you up, Lovell, you're hopeless," Cary yelled back.

Jim frowned. He didn't need cheering up. He was just fine. He'd been a real pussycat since coming back.

Yeah, and pigs fly, the voice of his conscience admonished.

Fine. So he'd been grouchy because he missed Crystal. But how could some *guy* cheer him up?

He only had a second or two to wait for his answer.

Jackson Alton stepped into the doorway. Jim had been half expecting a visit from the object of his Colorado search. What he wasn't expecting in a million years was that he'd ever see the person who followed Alton into the office. The one person he most—and least—wanted to see.

For a long tense moment, he and Crystal stared at one another, neither willing or perhaps able to break the contact. Then Jackson broke the stalemate by crossing to the desk, blocking their view of each other. He dropped a plastic bag containing a letter and envelope on the desk.

"It came to her at Laurel Glen from Loveland," Jackson said without preamble. "He's coming for her."

Crystal's brother and his resemblance to the Taggerts was still startling, especially those intense blue eyes. The man might look calm at first glance, but the rigid set of his shoulders and the pinched white look around his lips told the true story. And the anger had little to do with the letter. If Jackson Alton were any less controlled, Jim knew he'd be on the floor looking up.

"Look, let's get this out of the way. You must have heard I nearly arrested Cole for something he didn't do. I went to Colorado because I felt I owed him. But I moved as carefully as I did to protect your reputation."

"I don't care about my reputation in Torrence. They all know me. If they think I've done something wrong, it's their problem. I care that you—"

"Jackson." Crystal's voice cracked in the room.

"'...lied to my family,'' Jackson finished smoothly as if his sister hadn't spoken, but still Jim knew the hostility was a result of the lies he'd told Crystal. The hurt he'd dealt her.

"Fair enough. But right now we have your sister to protect. I'll inform my captain and he'll assign a detective to investigate."

"I thought you'd be the one to handle it." Jackson looked disappointed.

Jim shook his head, pulling out a form to record the complaint. "I'm riding a desk right now until the doctors okay me for full duty. I'll brief the officer assigned about what went down in Colorado."

Crystal, he noticed, looked relieved that she wouldn't have to deal with him. Jim tried not to let it hurt. He filled out the report then left them in his office, going directly to the captain.

Ten minutes later, having argued with Bellgetty till he was nearly blue, and with his med file cleared, Jim found himself on his way back to his office with Crystal's stalker still his problem. The captain had taken the position that he had knowledge of the case and a better idea of the way the perp thought. Jim had even tried telling him that Crystal didn't want him on the case. That she hated him. The only excuse he hadn't used was that his own feelings for her might get in the way. But he couldn't say the words aloud. Saying it might make it true and he couldn't love her. He just couldn't.

On his way back to his office, he saw Jackson Alton walking down the hall toward the men's room. Great. That left him to deal with Crystal alone. He stopped, looked heavenward and quipped, "Thanks a lot!" then wondered if sarcasm directed at the Lord was blasphemous.

Crystal turned when he entered his office. He tried not to look at her, concentrating on the far wall because it hurt to see hate looking back at him from those once soft onyx eyes. Oddly, he found it didn't hurt any less to feel her angry gaze burning into him as he walked around the back his desk. He sat, and thankfully she looked away. Except that hurt, too.

"I'm sorry, but you'll be stuck with me," he explained quietly. Tenderly. "I tried to have it assigned to someone you'd be more comfortable with, but we're shorthanded and Captain Bellgetty feels I already know the case."

"Lovely," she said, disgust rife in her tone.

"Crystal, I'm sorry for having to use that information you gave me about your brother. I never wanted to hurt you, and I certainly never lied to you about anything else. Everything I said and did, except that phone call to Cole and one trip to the library, was the truth. I even tried at dinner to get you talking about how Jack's leaving affected you rather than why he left. I admit I didn't try very hard, but I did try. And I never meant to kiss you. To lead you on. But I was very attracted to you. It had been a long time since I felt like that and I—"

Jim stopped talking, aware that her eyes, still not focusing on him, had drifted over his shoulder to the narrow credenza behind him against the wall. He swiveled in his chair and looked at the pictures that had captured her attention.

"My parents on their anniversary almost a year before my father died," he said, pointing at the five-by-seven. "The pilot with me in the next picture is my sister, Joy. That's George in the background. She named her Cessna George. She also flies helicopters. She used to be with the Civil Air Patrol. Now she works for the U.S. Park Service and she occasionally flies rescue missions. And she uses George to fly for Angel Flight on her days off. They transport sick kids and some adults to hospitals where then can get help."

"She sounds like an adventurer," Crystal said, her tone a little less brittle. "She's very pretty. What about the last picture?" She squinted. "Is that Joy, too?"

Jim reached out and picked up the picture nearest him. He stared down at Jessie's smiling face and his. Frozen in time, not a care in the world, he and his Jessie hadn't had a clue what awaited them.

"This is of me with Jessie on the day of our engagement party."

"And you claim nothing you said or did but that call was a lie? Does your fiancée know you kissed another woman? Or don't I count as a woman? Is that it?"

You count more than any sane man would have let you.

Jim handed the picture to her. He could see she didn't want to take it but, finally, she did. "You'll notice I was a lot younger then. I still believed in a love that lasted a lifetime. Jess was killed two weeks later."

Crystal started to reach for him, then looked again at Jess's picture and pulled back. "Oh, Jim, I'm so sorry. I should never have made that crack. What on earth is wrong with me?"

I hurt you.

"It's never made sense. Her being dead," he said instead, rather than risk her pride. "She was the most alive person I'd ever met." Jim smiled wistfully, remembering how they'd met. It was still a legend in the Riverside PD.

"We met in the police department gym during a martial arts demo. When the instructor paired us for an exercise, she laid me out on my back in two seconds flat." Jim grinned. "I used to say I fell in love literally. We coined it love at first toss."

"I envy her the opportunity to toss you on your backside. How did she die, if you don't mind talking about it?"

He stared into space. No, he didn't mind. It reminded him the folly of love and the pain it brought. "Remember I mentioned that my friend Greg was shot twice in the line of duty? The first time she was his partner and she was killed in the same exchange. It hurt so bad I thought I'd die, but I didn't. I vowed that day to never open myself to that kind of pain again. I can't. I won't go there again."

He managed to focus on her. "No matter how attracted I am to you. No matter how much I like you. I won't love you. Ever."

Crystal heard what Jim said for the warning she knew it was. And her heart broke all over again. For him. For his long-dead Jessie. For herself. She blinked back tears.

He liked her. He was attracted to her. He had not lied about that. She could see that now. But he also would never love her as she loved him. Once again, love had been stolen from her by grief. Jim would never give up his memories of Jessie for the possibility of building a life with her just as her father had never stopped hanging on to the past.

"Who asked you to love me?" she demanded, covering her heartbreak. She'd scrambled and begged for love her whole life and she refused to do it any longer. Not from Jim and not from her father. "Who even asked you to like me? My father asked for your help with this stalker but I didn't. Remember that."

Jim nodded. "Just see that you don't keep anything about the case from me again. No matter how furious you are at me. You would have been killed that last night at the Circle A if your father hadn't come home."

"I was going to tell Caleb in the morning."

"Too late. And if you'd come to me with the note, I would have told you the danger was probably immediate. I might even have caught this guy in the house. It's his pattern. Note. Event. Very little lag time."

She huffed out an annoyed breath. So she'd been wrong. "Fine. You'll be the first one I call. Just don't lie to me again and we'll get along perfectly."

"Ah. A truce has been effected," Jackson drawled from the doorway. "Am I to assume you're our investigator after all?"

Jim nodded. "Bellgetty hasn't got anyone else free. You need to watch her. So far, whenever she gets a note something happens. This guy could easily be here already. This was mailed three, maybe even four, days ago depending on how frequently they empty the mailbox it was sent from."

"Why wouldn't he have mailed it from here? I would think that would have turned up the fear. Been more immediate."

"Because he's also all about not getting caught. He's careful and smart. He could be coming via any airport in the country. It's a huge job to check on every passenger on every flight into Philly in a four-day period. And we don't know he's even here yet. There's also no guarantee that we'll recognize a name. He could have been in the Torrence area using an alias. We also don't know he flew here. Newark. LVI. Baltimore. They're all a relatively short drive from here."

"You've got nothing to go on?" Jackson asked, sounding even more worried as he came in and sat in the chair next to Crystal.

Jim opened the file and pulled out a piece of paper. "I contacted a profiler about this and got the results late yesterday. She says he's smart, careful, demented and extremely jealous. Probably college educated." Jim shrugged. "She also says he's extremely careful about his personal habits. Almost pathological about proving he's been close to her."

Crystal took in almost none of what Jim's profiler had reported. Her mind and heart were too wrapped up in the implications of what he'd done. He hadn't left this case behind him when he'd come home. He'd continued to worry about her. Then she remembered how much Jim loved solving mysteries.

He loved the mystery, not her.

"How did you get all that from a few notes? And what exactly is a profiler's job?" Jackson wanted to know.

"A profiler looks at evidence or the lack of it. Pattern. Wording of notes. The ultraclean paper and lack of any prints. The shell casings having been retrieved and any tracks obliterated from where he shot me. It all means something to these guys. They take what they see and build a personality so we can possibly narrow our search. A guy I went to school with is with the FBI. He did me a favor after I got back here and called in a marker with the bureau's profiler. Caleb faxed me everything we have so far and I sent it on."

Jim dropped the piece of paper back into the file. "In this case I don't see it helping. The profile doesn't fit anyone *I* met in Torrence. Sound familiar to either of you?"

"Nope," Jackson replied as Crystal shook her head. "What kind of protection can you provide?" her brother asked then.

"We'll step up patrols out that way. I'd suggest not taking on any new help till we get this settled. Don't go anywhere alone, Crystal. So far, there seems to be safety in numbers. He's after you, not those around you."

"He shot you," Jackson pointed out before she could.

"True, but I'd gotten in his way. He couldn't get near your sister because I was always with her. He also got jealous thinking there was something going on between us."

"Which proves he isn't as bright as your profiler says," Crystal quipped.

The joke fell flat.

"Yes. Well," Jim said, standing. "There's nothing more we can accomplish here today. I suggest you try to relax, Crystal. But don't leave her alone," he told Jackson, reaching out to shake his hand.

Jackson stood and took Jim's hand. "Thanks for trying with the profiler. I guess you'll be in touch."

Jim nodded and looked down at her. "I'm sorry for everything."

She knew he meant more than lying about his reason for the trip to Colorado. He meant his heartbreaking vow, too. She stood. That was the one thing she couldn't forgive. "Not a problem," she said, hiding the fact that it was a huge problem and hurried out of there before she told him how *much* of a problem it really was.

"I wish I could go home," she told Jackson on the way to the car. "Or better yet, disappear. Leave all this behind and just start over. I'm thoroughly sick of my entire life."

Jackson slung his arm around her shoulders. "It'll work out. The guy's nuts about you, and I'm not talking about the stalker."

"Are you crazy? The man's as bad as Dad. He has a dead fiancée in his past, just like Dad has Mama.

I'm not playing second fiddle to a memory ever again. No way. No how. End of discussion.''

Jackson didn't say anything but he didn't look convinced, either.

As Crystal walked along the aisle in Stable One, CJ Larson, Laurel Glen's trainer, called from inside a stall, ''Afternoon, Crystal.'' The sound of the unexpected voice made her jump and her heart pound. Two days had gone by since the note came. Nothing had happened. And Crystal was crawling out of her skin.

She almost turned around and left because she didn't want to deal with her mixed feelings for CJ. She liked the younger woman a lot, but she also made Crystal uneasy through no fault of her own. CJ was everything Crystal had always wanted to be and wasn't. Adorably delicate and short, with long blond hair and golden eyes. She was also perhaps the only woman Crystal had ever met with the potential to understand her completely. The dichotomy drove her crazy.

There was another big problem, as well. CJ was engaged to the man who'd asked Jim Lovell to investigate Jackson. Consequently, Crystal hadn't taken very well to Cole. She knew she hadn't given the admittedly affable scion of Laurel Glen a chance. When her heart was so battered, it was hard to forget the havoc he'd accidentally wreaked on her life. After all, if she hadn't met Jim, she wouldn't know what she was missing.

But now that she knew, now that she'd fallen in

love with him, she didn't know how to go back to the way it had been. The way *she* had been. Numb to feelings. Uninformed about possibilities. Frozen in place.

"Oh. Hi," Crystal said, and wished her voice didn't sound so uncertain. "Meg called and wanted me to meet her and Beth here."

"Beth? Oh, Elizabeth! I may never get used to Jack's nickname for her or you calling him Jackson for that matter."

"What can I say. He's always been Jackson. And Beth is perfect for him. She's so sweet and nice," Crystal said.

"Cole's sweet and nice, too," CJ ventured. "Kind of like a big gorgeous yearling. Clumsy sometimes, but with a heart just as big as he is. He might step on a few toes or nip at a few fingers by accident, but he never means for anyone to get hurt. In fact, he'd be more hurt emotionally than the person who accidentally got in his way."

CJ closed the stall door. "He ..um...he told me about asking Jim Lovell to investigate Jack. You have to understand, Jack's resemblance to the family made Cole nervous. He's also very protective of Elizabeth, and she'd started getting involved with Jack. Cole was worried about the people he loves. He wasn't trying to hurt anyone." She smiled. "He thinks you're going to deck him at the first opportunity and he just wishes you'd get it over with so we can all be friends."

Crystal chuckled and sat on a bale of hay. "I understand why he did what he did. It's just—" She stopped and sighed. "Oh, who am I trying to kid. Jim decided how to go about it. Not Cole. Tell him he's safe, okay?"

"Sure. And what about being friends?"

"Okay. I'll try to work on that, too. So when are you getting married?"

CJ frowned and crossed her arms. "Who knows? Maybe I'll let you deck him, after all. Cole's got it in his head that every woman wants a church wedding complete with a bridal gown and veil and brides-maids." She spread her arms. Blond and petite, CJ was dressed exactly like Crystal in jeans, work boots and a chambray shirt. "Do I look like the bridal-gown type?"

"You could wear anything you want and not look like an idiot. Imagine me in ruffles and flounces. I try getting dressed up like a woman and I look like the female version of a grown-up Baby Huey!"

A snicker she tried to hide escaped CJ. "Being short doesn't mean I have the first clue what to pick out to wear," CJ claimed diplomatically. "Elizabeth called my closet a denim explosion. She and Cole's sister dressed me up for a charity ball about a month ago. You can't imagine how much trouble it was. It took hours. I admit I kind of liked how I looked, but it just made Cole nervous."

"No, it knocked him for a loop or he wouldn't have panicked and acted like a fool," Beth said as she and Meg Taggert stepped into the stable through a side door.

Meg Taggert was the most incredible-looking fifty something woman Crystal had ever seen. She had dark eyebrows, impossibly long lashes framing the sapphire eyes she'd passed to her son. But her hair was her most startling feature. It was a rich shade of platinum white that couldn't have come out of a bottle. But when juxtaposed with her youthful face it was shocking at first glance. She drew all eyes whenever she entered a room.

And Beth was simply gorgeous, which had been Jackson's only description on the phone of the tall, willowy blonde with kind green eyes who had agreed to marry him. If Crystal had placed an order for a sister, Beth would have filled the bill perfectly.

"CJ, dear," Meg said, "you have yet to find something to wear to the engagement party on Saturday night. And I made us an appointment about a wedding gown."

CJ groaned. "Cole sicced you on me, didn't he?"

"No, dear boy that he is, he did not. Actually it was his sister, my wonderful niece, Hope, who I might add is at home with a very cranky baby, wishing she could come along with us. Don't we all feel lucky? Now come. The mall awaits."

No one moved as Crystal wondered why she'd been included in the shopping trip and how to gracefully get out of it. It wasn't as if she was family. Besides, why would they want to go shopping with her? Talk about mission impossible.

Then Beth spoke up. "Crystal, the engagement party is formal and Jackson says he didn't tell you to pack a gown."

"I wasn't planning to attend," she said, and wondered why Beth looked hurt.

"He did tell you it's not just for Cole and CJ but for him and Elizabeth, didn't he?" Meg asked.

No. He hadn't. Brothers! She'd have to kill him later. Crystal met CJ's still-horrified gaze and felt renewed kinship with the petite blonde. She grimaced. "CJ, I think we're going shopping."

Chapter Nineteen

Crystal knew the torture of clothes shopping wouldn't turn out to be fun as Meg and Beth had billed the trip to the mall. And it didn't. Even with three women she liked, shopping was still…torture!

They went to the huge King of Prussia Mall and Plaza complex, which included a dizzying selection of stores in two large malls. She'd have loved to idly wander through the crowds, looking in all the windows and admiring the many interesting and exotic shops. But Meg quickly pronounced that they were there on a mission and she would allow no stalling, so the torture began immediately.

CJ was, as Crystal thought, easy to buy for with major alterations planned for hemlines. After all, most major department stores carried petite clothes and there were eight big anchor stores between the two malls. Beth and Meg managed to find a full trousseau for CJ in just under two hours, but they'd failed in the ensuing three to find just one dress for Crystal.

Crystal was the only one not surprised. It had been the story of her life since age sixteen.

"Take it off," Meg pronounced with a flick of her wrist. "The only reason it's long enough is that it hangs on you. It's so matronly I wouldn't let my mother wear it if she were still alive. I don't understand this. You have a perfectly proportioned body, and I swear there's not an ounce of fat on you. What are these manufacturers thinking? This is simply infuriating."

Crystal couldn't say she disagreed. Maybe she would just stay behind at the little cottage that came with Jackson's position. She'd curl up with a good book. Or watch a movie. A perfect evening.

"This is one of the reasons I didn't bring much along. Big women's clothes are made for heavy women, not big and tall women."

"Wait," Beth said. "Where's my head? I know where we should look. There's a little tall shop up Route 202. It has gorgeous clothes. I forgot about it because it starts at the next size up from mine."

Crystal was sick of the whole thing. "But CJ still needs to find her wedding gown," she hedged, feeling just a bit guilty for prolonging CJ's own torture.

"Oh, that's okay," CJ piped up gaily. "You need something right now. The party's Saturday."

That instantly freed Crystal of any guilty feelings whatsoever. But there would be no triumph for either of them.

"I see what you two are up to," Meg cut in. "This is one of the reasons we came in separate cars. CJ, you and I have an appointment at three at Neiman's.

Surprise, I'm buying your wedding gown. Elizabeth, you can take Crystal up to the tall shop and buy her something stunning. And if you happen to see more, encourage this young lady to bolster the local economy. Remember this was the plan. You two did not divide and conquer.''

They left Meg and CJ arguing about the cost of a wedding gown, and fifteen minutes later Crystal followed Beth into the unassuming shop in a small strip mall. Her spirits had risen somewhat, energized by the hustle and bustle surrounding her. Life in the north was so invigorating. This is what she'd been missing on the ranch. Excitement! Life!

Then she looked around the shop as they entered and blinked. The racks were higher off the floor than in a regular store. The garments longer at a glance. Paradise!

''May I help you?'' a sales woman with gorgeous coffee-and-cream skin asked. Crystal actually had to look up a bit to meet her eyes. What a treat! And the dress she wore was as perfect as that one outfit she and Julia had stumbled upon in Greeley. Simple. Elegant.

''My brother's engagement party is this Saturday. It's formal,'' she told the woman.

''He didn't warn her before she flew out here. I love him but every once in a while he's such a *man*,'' Beth joked.

''In defense of my brother, he would think how I look doesn't matter to me.''

''Would he be wrong?'' Beth asked.

Crystal sighed. ''He'd be wrong. I wish I could be

glamorous. But you've seen it. Nothing ever fits right. Or looks right. Or they're styled like my grandmother would wear them so I won't. I know what I like but I can never find it.''

''Well, honey, you came to the right place,'' the clerk said cheerfully. ''We specialize in tall women. And I'd kill for that figure of yours. Let's look around and see what you think.''

Ten minutes later, Crystal stared at herself. ''Oh, my goodness.''

''You sound like Shirley Temple.''

She chuckled. ''If Jim were here, he'd probably know the movie name and the character she played. It's a game we played.'' The heartbreak of losing him caught her unawares and stole her breath. And looking like a fashion model didn't matter. Nothing mattered. Once again she found herself blinking back tears.

Beth must have seen her distress. ''Crystal, Jack says Lieutenant Lovell is just crazy about you. So why aren't you going after what you so clearly want?'' Beth asked.

Crystal turned to the side for another view of the teal dress. Its lines emphasized her flat stomach. She straightened a bit, refusing to wallow. ''Because I'm not a glutton for punishment. How much has Jackson told you about life with our father?''

Beth patted the seat next to her. ''See if sitting in it is comfortable.'' Crystal couldn't see the harm in that so she did. Then caught unaware, Beth bushwhacked her.

''Do you realize that by giving up on Jim Lovell

you're giving up on the possibility of a wonderful future? Jim warned you not to pursue him because he refuses to fall in love again. So you folded your tent and faded away. If Jack had given up on me that easily, I'd still be hiding behind a brittle facade and we'd be missing out on all the love we share.''

"It's Jim who won't give up the past.''

"I don't think so. Jim sounds as if he's afraid. So was I. But he *doesn't* sound as if he's still grieving for the policewoman who died. He kissed you. He acknowledged an attraction to you. Jack says your father still acts as if your mother died yesterday. Jim might be stuck by the past, but he's not stuck *in* the past. It's different. What have you got to lose by going after him and…and roping him and dragging him out of that place where he's stuck and into the present? You just might gain a bright future for a prize.''

Crystal grinned. ''Nice ranching metaphor. Are you practicing to be a rancher's wife?''

Beth just grinned and lifted her shoulders. ''I'll go where Jack goes.''

Thoughtful, Crystal stood staring at her reflection. Was Beth right? She *was* about the grief thing. Jim wasn't grieving. Her father had yet to smile at a memory, wistfully or not. Jim was just determined to avoid further pain. That was different from her father. Evan Alton wallowed in his pain and had made it a part of his life. Jim just ran from even the possibility of it. What *did* she have to lose?

She'd already lost her heart.

Determined, she stood and twirled a little. The narrow straps held up a draped neckline and a figure-hugging princess-line bodice that flared to the floor from the hips. Made of Chinese silk in a delicate pattern, it had a slight Asian flare with contrasting piping set in the seams and straps. She loved it!

"I love it!" she declared.

"So do I. So what else do we buy so you can shake up Lieutenant Lovell? If he could barely resist you in work clothes…" Beth waggled her perfect eyebrows, making Crystal laugh.

"It's dark already," Crystal said with no small amount of wonder as they left the store quite a while later—her bank balance reduced considerably but satisfyingly. She'd need another suitcase just to get her new wardrobe home. A year-round wardrobe since the summer things were on clearance and the fall lines were in already. She couldn't remember ever having so much fun.

"We've been working hard. Care to share a very late dinner?"

Crystal giggled. "I do believe, future sister-in-law, that is an excellent—" In the glow of the big parking lot lights, she spotted a piece of paper tucked under the driver's side windshield wiper. The block letters looked glued on even from where she stood. "What's that?" she asked, her voice as unsteady as her legs all at once.

"Probably just an advertisement," Beth said, reaching for it. She froze. "Oh, dear Lord. It's a threat, Crystal."

"We need to call Jim!"

"Okay. Sure. But let's do it on the way home,"

Beth said, a slight tremor in her voice. She went to unlock the door.

"No," Crystal said, remembering waking up behind the wheel on a lonely road. "He usually strikes right after leaving me a note. I learned my lesson with that near-gas explosion. Let's go right back inside the store. Jim said there's safety in numbers and the store had a guard. Come on."

Beth hesitated. "Jack, too. We'll call Jack, too?"

"It's okay, Beth. We'll call Jack. What does the note say?"

"'You took my love. Now you die.'"

Clutching the packages tightly as they reentered the store, Crystal turned to Beth. "How could I take someone's love who I don't know? How can anyone be this demented?" she cried.

Elizabeth shook her head, put down the bags she had and put her hand on Crystal's shoulder. "Lieutenant Lovell will figure it out. We have to believe that."

A bomb. Jim signed off from the local uniform at the scene. His brain felt as if it were about to explode and he could hardly breathe. Not very professional, he chided himself, but the guy had planted what looked like a bomb in Elizabeth Boyer's car.

Would it hurt less to lose Crystal now without having admitted to your love? a voice inside him demanded. It was a question with only one answer. With his heart pounding as he skirted up the shoulder of the road, lights flashing, Jim admitted the truth and he did it out loud. "No, it wouldn't. It might even hurt more."

"You brought her into my life, Lord. Please help me keep her safe. And thank You for Crystal's wisdom in not starting for home."

Minutes later and somewhat calmer, Jim wheeled into the lot of the strip mall and screeched to a halt outside the crime scene tape Jim assumed they'd put up to keep bystanders at a safe distance. He noticed that Jack had arrived already and had his arms around both women.

Jack must have noticed Jim, as well, because he let go of Crystal and Elizabeth and met him halfway across the lot.

"The bomb squad's on the way," he told Crystal's brother.

"I want protection for her, Lovell—24/7. Do I need to hire somebody? I could have lost both my fiancée and my sister. Beth didn't want to wait here. Suppose Crystal had given in?"

Jim couldn't contemplate that and kept his wits about him. He ran a hand through his hair and hoped Jack didn't notice the tremor. "Done already. He's on the way. I'm going to figure this out, Jack." His voice shook and Crystal's brother blinked.

"Okay. Meanwhile, I want to take them home. They're both pretty shaken up."

Glancing toward Crystal, Jim felt his heart flip. He wanted so desperately to hold her, comfort her, but knew he had to get his mind off his feelings for her and on to the case. There was something he was missing. Something they were all missing. He just had to figure it out.

Jim nodded. "Yeah. Take them home." He turned when a second set of lights flashed into the lot. "There's your escort now."

"Maybe you should go talk to Crystal. Tell her how you feel," Jack suggested.

"Gave myself away, huh?" Jim asked, grinning.

"You were white as a ghost when you got out of that car. The shaking hand and voice were pretty good tip-offs, too."

"I can't tell her here like this. I'll be by tomorrow. Tonight, though, I'm going over it all again. There has to be something we're not seeing. Some little slip-up."

Jack reached out and shook his hand. "Thanks for the protection, and good luck."

Jim stayed where he was and watched them drive away with the cruiser trailing them. The trooper he'd requested was conscientious and quick-witted. Crystal would be safe at Laurel Glen.

Jim sat in his living room at dawn the next morning still staring at the files he'd been going through all night. He started at the beginning once again, sifting through everything in the files. When nothing new occurred to him, he went through it mentally again.

It had started in a small town in Colorado where everyone knew everyone else. Now it had moved here. He had Cary Stephens checking flight records against the Torrence and Loveland phone books. So far—nada!

It was so frustrating. You'd think someone in a town that size would have seen something suspicious, yet Caleb and Joe King had talked to everyone they could think to question.

Maybe that was the wrong approach. What about anyone they couldn't question? What about anyone not in town?

He picked up the phone and called Colorado. "Hi, Mirabel. It's Jim Lovell."

"Are you aware, young man, that it's five in the morning here?"

Jim looked at his watch and winced. Mirabel worked at home from six to six. No one called during those hours unless it was an emergency. Well, as far as he was concerned that's what this was. "Sorry, but we had another attempt on Crystal last night. I've been up all night trying to put this together. Can you get hold of either Hart or King? I need them to see if anyone has left town. Can you have them do that?"

"Is Cris all right?"

"Crystal's fine so far. I want to keep it that way. Has anyone you know of got experience with explosives?"

"Explosives?"

"Yeah. Someone planted a bomb in a car she was riding in. It was wired to the ignition. If they'd started the car, both women would have been killed."

"My, my. I don't know of anyone fool enough to fool with such things. I'll add that to the boys' checklist, though. How should they reach you?"

"Call my cell. Thanks, Mirabel."

Deciding maybe a nap and a shower might sharpen his wits, he headed for the bedroom. Even though his mind was going around and around, he drifted off from sheer exhaustion.

Chapter Twenty

Crystal rinsed the last of the breakfast dishes then sat back down with her cup of coffee. She kept going back in her mind to the night before. Jim hadn't even come over to talk to her. It had hurt as much as hearing the phone call to Cole because she'd desperately needed his comfort. She could close her eyes even now and remember the feel of his arms surrounding her the night he'd found her on that lonely road. He'd made her feel safe and secure for the first time since Grandmother died.

But that was then.

Here in Pennsylvania, he'd sent her home with her brother. He hadn't even bothered to cross the lot to see how she was doing. Jackson said Jim was frustrated and very concerned. He said Jim promised to be out to see her today, but that he'd had to stay at the scene.

Jackson had tried to divide his attention between her and Beth all night, but Crystal had felt like a fifth wheel. So to give them time alone, she'd claimed to be exhausted and had gone to bed. She slept fitfully with strange dreams waking her periodically.

This morning, before Jackson went off to work, he'd said Beth had stayed at Laurel House rather than go home alone. He'd explained that Beth had been raped as a young teen and that Crystal's situation had shaken her more perhaps than it would someone else.

"Hello," Beth called through the screen door.

Crystal jumped up. "Beth. Come on in. I was just thinking about you. How are you doing?"

"I was about to ask you the same thing. Jack said to tell you he'd be here for lunch. I thought maybe you'd like to go for a ride."

Before she could answer, the phone rang. "Hello," she said, answering it.

"Hi. Guess who this is?"

"Julia! It's so good to hear your voice."

"Likewise. Remember that convention I was trying to get the town council to spring for? Well they did!"

"Then you're in Philadelphia?"

"Sure am. I hoped we could meet somewhere near here. They have the most fabulous restaurants in this city. Rusty's Place is never going to live up to this. So can you meet me?"

"Actually, I'd better not. He's here, Jule. He followed me and I'd never forgive myself if something happened to you because of me."

"How could he be here? No one knew where you were going. I'll bet that stupid, ignorant Joe King let it slip when he was going around town, playing at being a detective."

"Or he guessed since Jim left at the same time."

"I guess that's possible. Are you all right?" her friend asked.

Crystal leaned back against the kitchen counter. "So far. But Jackson's fiancée, Beth, was with me last night. It was pretty scary."

"Jackson's getting married? That's great, but what happened last night? Is she hurt badly?"

Hearing a near-hysterical edge making its way into Julia's voice, Crystal hastened to explain. "Oh, no. Nothing happened to either of us. In fact, she's here with me now. There was a bomb in the car, but he left a note and an angel on my shoulder told me to call for help and not start the car. Jim. Jim told me there was a pattern and to get help right away if I got another note. So I guess he was the angel."

"Unlikely angel though he is, thank heaven you listened to him." There was a long pause. "Oh... Now I really want to see you just to see for myself that you're all right. Maybe I could rent a car. That can't be too hard. Can you tell me how to get there?"

"No, but I'll bet Beth can." She turned to Beth. "Can you give directions to Julia?"

Beth got on the phone and gave Julia directions. It was nice to have something to concentrate on besides her misery over Jim and her fear of the man stalking her. Beth offered Julia a tour of Laurel Glen when she got there and the three planned to eat lunch at Jackson's little kitchen table.

It took Julia nearly three hours, but they finally heard her pull into the spot next to Jackson's cottage. Julia bounded out of the little rented compact and hugged Crystal tight. "I've been so worried, but you look just fine." Julia giggled. "Goodness, driving in that city was something else."

Jule had always reminded Crystal of an excitable terrier when she was worked up. "I told you we were fine. Julia Winter, meet Beth Boyer, soon to be Beth Alton."

"Your directions were perfect." She hugged Beth, clearly taking her by surprise. "Oh, but this is so exciting! Our Jackson getting married."

"Will you still be here Saturday? Maybe you could come to our engagement party," Beth generously offered. "Jack's father can't make it and I know he'd just love to have someone else from his hometown to celebrate with him."

"That's so sweet of you, but I don't have anything fancy enough."

Crystal laughed. "How do you know you'd need a fancy dress? Maybe it's a barbeque?"

Julia blushed. "I guess I've watched *The Philadelphia Story* one too many times. I saw the house. It just doesn't say barbeque."

"Don't listen to Crystal's teasing," Beth said. "She's as bad as her brother. Saturday *is* formal but we're pretty relaxed around here. Whatever you have with you would be just fine."

"That isn't what I heard. I had to buy a dress," Crystal teased.

"Where *is* Jackson?" Julia asked.

"Working somewhere on the property," Crystal explained. He's foreman here. And Jule, he's so happy in his job. We'll see him eventually."

"Would you like that tour or do you want to freshen up and eat first?" Beth graciously asked.

Crystal couldn't believe how out of it she was today. "You're so much better a hostess than I am, Beth. So, Jule, what's your pleasure?"

"I want that dollar-tour Beth promised. I want to see everything that makes this different from a ranch. Besides, with this sticky heat, freshening up later makes more sense."

"Come and learn, grasshopper," Crystal teased. She drew a giggle from Julia, but had to fight a wave of sadness. That was one of Jim's lines.

They walked though the stables and gawked at the different horses, Julia peppering Beth with numerous but intelligent questions.

"Is there any way I can get to see anyone use the jumps and such?"

"I board my horse here. Her name is Glory. She's a seven-year-old Irish Draught horse." Beth smiled that sweet smile Crystal just knew had stolen her brother's heart. "And I bet I can convince her to put on a show."

Minutes later, Elizabeth, having explained the difference in English and Western tack, stood ready to mount in the big circular exercise ring. She looked around. "You know, I wonder where everyone is?"

"Could that have something to do with it?" Julia asked, pointing south. They both turned to look at smoke billowing up from behind one of the rolling hills.

"I'd better go take a look. Can I get a leg up, Crystal?" Beth asked.

And then just as Crystal felt Beth catapult into the saddle, Glory exploded like a demented wild thing screaming. The gray horse reared and Julia ran. Time slowed, and Crystal watched in horror as Beth flew out of the saddle and under the pawing hooves. Crystal yelled a warning for Beth to get up and run but she didn't move. Not thinking of her own safety but of Jackson's face when he looked at his ladylove, Crystal charged forward, waving her arms. She heard Julia yelling that she shouldn't try to help Beth, when the world exploded into a rainbow of lights. Then darkness fell and so did she, never hearing the siren screaming up the long drive.

Jim's cell phone rang at noon and he bounded up out of bed, horrified he'd slept so long. He scrambled for the ringing phone. "Lovell," he said.

"Jim. It's Caleb Hart. I've got to tell you King isn't a happy camper today, thanks to you. We've had Mirabel on the phone since dawn calling everyone around here. So far, everyone is present and accounted for except Julia Winter, but of course she goes to see her aunt on weekends a lot."

Jim sighed. "Yeah. Crystal mentioned that. Thanks for checking to see if everyone was accounted for. It was a shot in the dark, but what can I say? Desperation's setting in."

He dropped onto the sofa in front of the reports and copies of the threatening note he'd left spread all over the coffee table.

"I can imagine you are desperate by now," Caleb said. "And the answer to the other question is, no.

Neither of us can think of anyone who knows how to build a bomb like the one Mirabel described to us.''

Jim heard the answer, but his mind was on the second note planted in Crystal's purse. The one she'd found the night before they flew to Philly. There was something wrong with it and Jim suddenly knew what it was. "Caleb? What's mauve?"

"Mauve? Some sort of color. Right?"

"Yeah. But do you know how to describe it? Better yet, if you saw it, would you know to call it that?''

"No. Why?''

Uneasiness ground at his stomach. "Neither would I. It's generally a female word. Women know various shades, but for the most part, men don't. I need you to call Julia's aunt. Find out if she's there. And find out what kind of car the aunt drives.''

"Julia? That's pretty far-fetched. They're best friends.''

"I know. But check. And check her house.''

Jim could hear Caleb calling it in on his car radio. "I'm on my cell, so stay with me,'' the deputy said. "Her place is only a block and a half away.'' The radio squawked in the background. "Mirabel says Julia isn't at her aunt's. And her aunt broke her hip so she hasn't used her car. It fits our paint color and it's one of the possible model years. She's hobbling out to the garage… Damage! She swears when she parked it in there it was fine.''

"Don't go inside Julia's place,'' Jim told Caleb. "If you find anything, it won't be admissible.''

"Way ahead of you. That's one nice thing about a

small town. The judge lives three houses down from her. Give me five minutes and I'll have a warrant.''

"I'm making tracks for Jack's place at Laurel Glen. Call me on this number.''

Jim tore out of the house and almost dove into the car. He whipped out onto the street while mounting his light and flipping on his siren. As he screamed along, he called Crystal. He needed to warn her and probably convince her the stalker was Julia since her friend's guilt made no sense. But Crystal's phone rang until it went to the answering machine.

"Crystal, sweetheart, I know this isn't going to make any sense, but it's Julia. I don't understand it, either, but I just know it's her. Be careful.''

Next he called the trooper who was supposed to be watching Crystal. He didn't answer, either, and Jim's heart pounded harder. She had to be all right.

Please, Lord. Let her be safe. I've never told her how I feel. What if something happens to her?

Jim tried Jackson's office number and got his machine there, too. Cole would be at his office, but that was farther away than Jim was already. The only other number he had was for Laurel House. He tried that and got a maid who told him there was a fire in one of the hay fields and that everyone was there trying to stop it. He prayed Crystal was there, as well. It was the same diversion Julia had used in Torrence to keep Crystal alone on that road.

After hooking up the hands-free mode on his cell phone, Jim pressed his foot to the floor. He knew in his heart that seconds counted. He careened around a corner and onto Indian Creek Road. The back end fishtailed, but he held it to the road.

He was now about five minutes from Laurel Glen when the phone rang and Jim answered.

"Jim. It's Caleb. I got a warrant."

"And?" he asked, but somehow knew he was right.

"She's one burnt cookie. Only, I don't see why she's after Crystal."

"What do you have?"

"The small bedroom. It's a shrine. To Jackson. Snapshots blown up to poster size. Football trophies made to look like the ones I know he earned. His jersey. Books that were his, with his name scrawled inside. I guess she stole them. This is weird. I don't get it. She has a thing for Jackson? So why go after his sister?"

It made sense to Jim. "No wonder we couldn't pin it down. It's been a smoke screen all along to get Jack to come home to offer support to Crystal. Julia's been nagging her for weeks to call Jack and tell him she needed him."

"And now?" Caleb asked.

You took my love. Now you die. "She isn't after Crystal. Now she's gunning for Jack's fiancée."

Chapter Twenty-One

Jim drove past Laurel Glen's stables and saw Julia up ahead running toward the foreman's cottage. She was alone.

He caught up just as she reached her car. She'd almost gotten into the driver's seat when Jim grabbed her arm and hauled her back out. She went from mouse to monster in a split second, driving her fist into his bad arm. But he was beyond physical pain and thankful she hadn't tried to play innocent, wasting vital time.

"Where's Crystal?" he demanded as he slapped a cuff around her wrist. She was so slim, her wrist almost slipped through the bracelet. She was small, but she had caused big trouble.

Julia looked up at him, her pale blue eyes fevered and a lot less than sane. "Crystal didn't listen," she hissed. "She never listens to anyone! I have to go. You have to let me go." She pulled against the cuff. Tried to wriggle away. "I have to find Jackson. He'll need me now that his precious Beth is dead. Now that they're both dead. He'll finally need me.''

She'd killed them? Jim felt his heart crack and was almost distracted enough to miss her other hand moving toward his arm. He grabbed that wrist just in time to stop a horse-size hypo from sinking into him. It took more effort than he'd have thought to wrestle it out of her hand. And a bit more to get her arms behind her so he could cuff them around the door frame.

''Where are they?'' he demanded again as he crushed the second cuff closed.

''Glory,'' she giggled. Her voice a singsong travesty, she sang, ''Glory sent them to glory.'' Her laughter was uncontrolled and hysterical.

Jim backed away, his heartbeat throbbing in his ears. He looked back down the drive and jumped back behind the wheel, heading for the stables where he thought Julia had been.

Please, Lord, don't let me be too late.

He used his cell phone to check on the backup he'd called for and for an ambulance as he wheeled around the tight curve of the bluestone drive, spraying gravel in his wake. He jumped out when he got as far as the exercise ring that lay between all four stables. What he saw was a sight right out of his nightmares.

A gray horse stood between the prone figures of two women. Crystal and Elizabeth lay like broken dolls. Neither woman moved. The animal shook, and snorted, tossing its head.

''Tell them to come in silent,'' he told the dispatcher he still had on the line. Jim had noticed Cole's

SUV in the lot as he'd passed so he made one more call. This one was for more immediate help.

"Just listen," Jim said when Cole Taggert answered. "Crystal and Elizabeth are unconscious in the exercise ring. Glory, I think the horse is called, is standing between them. She's been drugged and is really wild-looking. Get here." He hit the power button and tossed the phone onto the seat. He was going into that ring and he didn't need it ringing and spooking the already-spooked horse.

His heart pounding, Jim opened the gate and stepped inside the ring. Never taking his eyes off the horse, he took one step then another, moving toward the center of the ring. Toward the women.

He was about twenty feet from Crystal's prone body when a noise behind him startled the horse. Glory pawed the ground, snorting and quivering, her hooves inches from Elizabeth's head.

"Get out of the way, Lovell. I'm going to have to put her down," Ross Taggert said, his voice controlled, but just a touch haunted.

"But which way is she going to fall? On Elizabeth or on Crystal? Besides, it isn't her fault."

"She's no less dangerous. I'm sorry as I can be but the women have to come first."

Jim nodded as Elizabeth moaned and started pushing her shoulders off the ground. Glory flinched and moved toward Crystal, the mare's hooves now dangerously close to her long vulnerable back.

Then Jack's voice unexpectedly whispered softly from off to his left. "Hold still for a second, Beth. Take stock. Can you feel your toes?" His voice was calm, but Jim knew he had to be scared out of his wits. Jim sure was.

Elizabeth nodded almost imperceptibly but, still, the movement had Glory's muscles bunching—quivering. The mare looked about ready to explode.

"Is anything tingling?" Jack was asking his Beth in that quiet almost not-even-there tone he'd used before. "Don't move. Just whisper."

"No. I'm fine," she murmured.

Glory cocked her head as if, through a drug-induced haze, the voice meant something.

Jim took another careful step while the animal was distracted by her master's voice. He could see blood pooling on the corral floor beneath Crystal's head.

Even minor head wounds bleed a lot, he told himself. *Please, Lord. Please let her be all right.*

"That's good, honey," Jack was saying. "Glory's not herself. She's on your right between you and Crystal. I need you to roll to your left. Can you do that? Can you roll real nice and slow and give our girl a little breathing room?"

Jim knew if she moved far enough, Ross could and would take the poor animal out. It seemed so unfair, but Ross was right. Crystal and Elizabeth were more important.

Elizabeth lifted herself onto her shoulders and slowly picked up her head. "Glory," she whispered, drawing the quivering animal a step closer to herself. Jack sucked an audible breath, Ross hissed and Jim took another cautious step forward, able now to see that Crystal was still breathing. Ross, meanwhile kept the rifle trained on the drugged horse.

Jim let his eyes circle the ring and saw that Cole Taggert and CJ Larson were slowly, carefully moving in toward the center of the ring from opposite sides.

"Jim, I know you want to pull her to safety but we shouldn't move her," Cole said, his voice so soft and calming Jim almost didn't recognize it. "Let me see what I can do with Glory."

"Just do something," Jim hissed back. "There's blood under her head."

"I'm on it, Studly Do-Right," Cole quipped as he smoothly stepped between him and Glory. He kept up the running patter to the horse who was clearly mesmerized by the sound of his voice. He inched closer and closer and Glory backed away from Cole a couple of steps—thankfully away from both Crystal and Elizabeth.

Elizabeth, meanwhile, got slowly to her feet and stepped into Jack's waiting arms. He held on to her, as if his life depended on it. Jim knew how he felt.

Able now to get to Crystal without spooking Glory into hurting her worse, Jim sank down next to her, praying the ambulance would get there. Praying she'd snap at him to let her up. Praying she'd at least open her eyes and spit in his.

She didn't move.

But still he prayed. What else could he do besides be ready to scoop her up out of danger if need be? He didn't know how long he knelt there, with his hand on her back feeling—willing—each breath she took. Then Jack pulled on his arm, telling him to let the ambulance crew move her, transport her.

Jim got to his feet, becoming aware of his surroundings. He looked around. The horse was being carefully led by CJ and Cole toward the animal clinic in the barn. Ross Taggert stood with his wife, the rifle leaning on the stable wall behind him. Elizabeth, with Meg Taggert standing attendance, sat on the back of the paramedic van being checked by one of the medics.

Feeling more than a little desperate, Jim looked at Jackson. "I never told her, Jack. I didn't get here in time and I never got to tell her."

"You will."

"You think?"

"Hey, ask anyone who's ever tangled with that girl. She has the hardest head around." Jack put his arm around Jim's shoulders. "Crystal's tough. She'll be fine. She has to be."

Except, Jim knew, she didn't have to be, not at all. He could lose her so easily. Life was so much more fragile than it looked sometimes.

At the hospital, Jim felt alone in the midst of the Taggert clan. It wasn't their fault. They tried to include him in on their prayers, but he was restless and needed to move. Hospitals always did this to him. To him they were a place of loss. Tommy Peterson. Jessie. His father.

He didn't want to be alone, but he didn't feel he belonged with the Taggerts as they supported one another in their worry for Jack's sister. She'd only been at Laurel Glen a week and a half, but they all loved her already. He didn't know why he was surprised by that. Hadn't he fallen in love with her just as fast and even more deeply?

Jim stood and paced into the hallway, looking for a doctor to ambush but the hall was empty. Why were they not telling him anything but that she was unconscious? It had been four hours. Her father was already on his way, but still they said they were running tests. That they'd know something soon.

He walked down to the chapel and went inside to pray. Maybe alone he'd find the words. He dropped into a pew and just let his mind drift. He could feel the Lord trying to comfort him even though he couldn't put his need into concrete thoughts. But then a vision of her, so pale and still as the helicopter lifted off, stole any peace his wordless prayers gained for him.

Getting to his feet, he turned to leave and found Greg Peterson standing there.

"I got a hold of Joy," Greg said, pushing away from the doorjamb. "She's in the middle of an Angel Flight. She said she's sorry she couldn't get here any sooner than later tonight."

"At least she's doing someone some good."

"As in you didn't do your warrior princess any good? That isn't what I hear. I hear you went into that ring with a horse you knew was probably drugged out of its mind. You're terrified of horses."

"Not so much anymore. Crystal taught me to ride so I could go on a roundup with her." He smiled wistfully, thinking of those days with her. "I got to like it."

"Miracles do happen. But come on. You can't tell me you weren't scared to death in that ring."

"Only for Crystal and Beth. Why couldn't I see it till it was too late?"

"See what? That it was a woman? The woman they arrested. That it was Crystal's friend. From what you told me, there were three other cops working on this case and one profiler. None of them made this Julia Winter as the perp, either. I hear two of them grew up with her along with Crystal and her brother. They all missed it."

He shook his head. "She taught me it was okay to love again. That it really is better to love and lose than not to love at all. But I never got to tell her."

"She knows."

"No. No, she doesn't. I told her I would never love her. And last night when I could have gone to her and told her I did, I waited. I was trying to figure out who was after her. I thought being even closer to her would get in the way."

Greg gestured for him to sit back down so Jim sat. It was movement of a sort and at least it wasn't a decision he had to make. He dropped his head against the wall behind him and Greg settled next to him.

"I can't even pray," Jim admitted.

Greg's hand covered his and squeezed. "Just rest in the Lord. He knows your heart and He knows your needs. You know He does." Jim nodded. "Angel sent a message," Greg continued. "I'm not sure what she meant. She said, 'Letting go is sometimes the greatest act of faith there is.'"

Jim nodded. He knew what Greg's wife meant. All

those years ago when Jim was still fighting God's call, he'd berated her for her simple "Thy will be done" prayer, as they'd followed the ambulance carrying Greg to the hospital. He sighed and closed his eyes. He just wasn't there yet.

"Hey, Super Cop," Jim heard Cole say. "The docs want a powwow. Jack wants you there." Jim checked his watch. About an hour had passed. Another hour of unconsciousness. No matter how you looked at it, that wasn't good.

"Is she...?"

"Still out but alive. Come on. Let's see what he has to say before we speculate. Elizabeth and Jack asked me to sit in." He shrugged as if to say, "Go figure." "Seems they think my medical knowledge could be a help."

Jim stood as Cole sauntered back into the hall. "Cole, thanks for what you did with the horse. And for sending me off to meet Crystal. I know that wasn't the intent but... Thanks."

"Why? Seems to me you're in a world of hurt right now and I'm the one who sent you there."

"But that's the point. It's worth it. What little time there was, at least I had that."

Cole stared at him as if digesting what he'd said in personal terms. "Yeah. It would be. Let's go see what the brains have come up with."

"The brains" as Cole called them, had come up with a big fat zero. They had no idea why Crystal remained unconscious. Which was good because there was no evidence of bleeding on the brain or a blood clot. And bad, because there was no way to know how long she'd be unconscious, why she was or if she'd ever wake. Brain damage was still a possibility. Some things were still a mystery to them, they said. And the brain was the biggest mystery of all.

They were encouraged to sit with her. Talk to her. He and Jack—the closest to her—were elected to take turns.

Jack went first, so Jim paced outside the ICU.

Thinking.

Thinking of all those bad possibilities for Crystal.

Waiting.

Waiting for the chance to just sit at her side. He could close his eyes and remember riding at her side. Learning about her world and listening to her yearn for something that sounded more like his.

What he yearned for now and truthfully yearned for then was to look on her beloved face. But he'd been such a coward. And now all he wanted was a chance to tell her all the things he should have understood sooner. Admitted sooner. Said sooner.

What he yearned for now was a second chance.

It was the one thing he knew he couldn't ask for because he finally understood what "Thy will be done" meant.

Jim stepped into the small glass room an hour later, his eyes riveted on the dark-haired angel lying so still in the bed. The antiseptic smell, the constant beep of monitors, the whir of an IV drip machine all assaulted his senses and caused a knot the size of his fist to tighten inside him. All day long he'd been forced to confront one personal nightmare after another. And with the Lord's help he'd handled every one.

And this was the final one. The hardest one. He sat at Crystal's side and took her hand. He ran his fingertips across its silky soft back then turned it over to trace the calluses left there by the hard day-in and day-out work she did.

Then before he lost his nerve, and swallowing against tears he couldn't hold back, he said the words he'd once railed against, "Thy will be done, Lord. You know what's best for her. You'll get me through. And I won't hide from life—from love—ever again. Jessie wouldn't have wanted it and Crystal would probably clobber me for it. I can't be any less brave than they. With Your help I can do it, Lord."

Chapter Twenty-Two

Crystal heard Jim's voice at the end of the dark hall. She was really too tired to get up and besides, she had a really bad headache. She guessed that was why she'd decided to take a nap.

"I just wish you'd open those beautiful angel eyes for me," he said, and she'd swear she heard tears in his voice.

Well, okay. If her waking up meant that much, maybe she would. After all, she'd waited for him to stop by all day because he'd told Jackson he would. She certainly didn't want to give up the chance to at least look at him. He really was awfully nice to look at. Maybe she'd even get up the energy to clobber him as he'd just suggested.

With a lot more effort than she'd have thought, Crystal wedged her eyes open. And confusion replaced everything else she had on her mind. She felt as if she was looking at a picture but it had major pieces missing. A puzzle as yet unfinished.

The room was all wrong. Her little room in Jackson's cottage was tree shaded and painted a muted, moss-green. This room was glaringly bright. All glass and metal and bright, bright white walls.

Jim was there. Right there. Not down the hall at all. He was sitting next to her. She hadn't dreamed his voice out of her desperate subconscious. And those *had* been tears she'd heard. He was crying. Staring at her and crying.

"Crystal?"

It confused her. Frightened her. Jim crying that way. And now her head felt as if it was going to explode. Plus Jim didn't look much better than she felt. "You look like you've had a really bad day," she said in a surprisingly rusty voice.

Jim hastily wiped away the tears that had tracked down his cheeks. Those terribly confusing tears.

"Hey, you. You decided to wake up," he said, sounding more uncertain than she could ever remember him sounding, yet beautifully gentle, too. "Welcome back."

"I figured you wanted me awake or you wouldn't be here talking out loud next to my bed." Why was she so muzzy-headed? "Don't tell my brother this— he's gone all protective and nervous about me all of a sudden—but I have a killer headache. I feel like I got kicked by a horse."

Click! A piece of the puzzle fell into place.

"Oh! I did, didn't I? That's why you look so worried." Her heart fell. "I guess that's the only reason you're here."

He kissed her hand. Actually picked it up and kissed it while staring at her as if she might disappear in a puff of smoke. "I'm here because I don't want to be anywhere else, angel. I'm sorry I ever let you think anything else."

"Angel?"

"That's the first thought that popped into my head when you smacked into me on the sidewalk in front of Rusty's. That you looked exactly the way I always thought an angel would look." He smiled a sweet, gentle smile. "My friend Greg calls you my warrior princess. I kind of think he called it right."

She smiled. She couldn't help it. He said the nicest things. She couldn't wait till he saw her in that great dress Beth had helped her find.

Snick! Another puzzle piece.

"Beth! Glory went wild. She threw Beth. Is she all right?"

"She's fine, thanks to you. You tried to help her."

"And Julia. Did Jule get away?"

Jim frowned. "No. I caught her. A lot of good that did you and Beth."

"Caught her? She fell? When she was trying to get out of the ring? I didn't see her fall or you arrive. At least, I don't remember that. Is she all right?"

Something she'd said deepened Jim's frown. He didn't look like a happy camper all of a sudden.

"I should call a doctor," Jim said, popping up off the stool, near panic invading his expression. "And Jack! Wow. Jack's been so worried." He dragged a hand through his hair. "I should have told him the second you woke up. What's wrong with my head? He only went out into the waiting room so I could come in and sit with you."

Waiting room? Crystal looked around. *Snap!* Yet

another piece. She was in the hospital. That hadn't occurred to her. The picture was clearer still. Pretty well complete.

"I'll be right back," Jim promised, and was true to his word, barely sticking his head out the door to alert the nurse. But a doctor rushed in and asked him to leave. He cast her a helpless look and closed the door behind him.

A ten-minute examination followed, during which time she had to answer a lot of dumb questions such as who the president was and what color the sky was. She not so patiently counted his fingers and had a little fun watching his eyes bug out when she squeezed them on command.

Crystal watched Jim carefully the whole time through the glass partition. At one point, Jackson was there but he shook his head, clapped Jim on the shoulder and left again. She knew Jim hated hospitals and that was evident in the way he paced, his back tense, his hand raking his hair again and again. The doctor finished finally and told her she'd be fine, but that she needed to stay in the hospital for observation for a day, or at most, two.

She sighed in resignation, prepared to shoo Jim out of there.

It was great that he was there. That he said he wanted to be there. Maybe he wasn't so afraid of the idea of them anymore. Maybe they had a chance. But that could be settled later when he wasn't a near basket case.

But first, she needed him to answer her question about Julia. If something had happened to her friend, she needed to know. And really, she needed to know if there had been any progress on the whole stalker thing. She smiled at the irony of her being hurt so innocently when there was someone out there who wanted her dead.

"I got elected to come back in," Jim said.

Oh. Elected. Maybe he was only being nice again. How many times could a heart break anyway?

"Well, don't let me keep you. I guess you have police things to do. My stalker to catch. Will that nice guard you had watching the house from his car be in a chair outside my door now?"

Jim straddled the stool and took her hand. She blinked, his touch made her want to cry.

"No. That nice guard is in the hospital, but he won't need to guard you. And I told you *here* is the only place I want to be."

"You said elected."

"Oh, no. Elected to tell you. About Julia."

"She's hurt?"

Jim pursed his lips. "She's in the county lockup, Crystal. It was Julia."

Crystal blinked. Confused. The puzzle scrambled again. Worse this time. "What was Julia? County lockup? Isn't that like jail?"

"The one calling, sending notes, everything. It was Julia." He held her hand tighter, as if trying to give her his strength. As if she needed it.

"That was a man. He was jealous. He shot you. Accused me of—"

Jim shook his head. Maybe she needed to borrow his strength. Julia wasn't her best friend but she was her only close friend besides her brother.

"All Julia," he said, and she could tell he hated

telling her this. "And the attempts here weren't about you at all," he went on, his tone infinitely gently. "She'd switched her focus. She was after Beth now. It was all about your brother. 'You took my love. Now you die.' She was obsessed with him. Remember how she kept telling you to call him? She was trying to get you to make him come home. I imagine she was even skewing those notes to point at Joe King. It worked for a while, didn't it?"

He kissed her fingers, staring into her eyes. His deep dark gaze said he understood that this was a blow. "When you refused one time too many to call Jack, she decided to kill you by blowing up the house. My partner has been to her hotel room. He found all sorts of info she pulled down off the Internet. Like how to make that bomb we found in Beth's car. And earlier today Caleb Hart got a search warrant for her house. She had a room—a shrine to Jack. The walls were covered with poster-size pictures of him, trophies that are copies of the ones he'd earned, books he'd used in high school that had his name written inside. It really creeped Caleb out."

Crystal felt chilly suddenly. It creeped her out, too. Julia. Her eyes filled with tears as she remembered the frightened little girl she'd seen hiding in the school yard that first day of school. She remembered taking her by the hand and telling her everything would be all right. She couldn't make this all right.

"What did she do to Beth's horse? I don't understand."

Jim took the sheet and dried her tears. "I'm so sorry, sweetheart. She used some kind of drug on Glory. Cole told me the name but it's as long as your arm. She took the trooper coffee. Said it was from you. It was drugged. He'll be fine. He's mostly feeling stupid now that the effects are wearing off. We all feel stupid. Me most of all. I'd been looking at what eventually tipped me off since the night she tried to blow up your house.''

''You—you figured it out?''

''I was probably two minutes late getting to you. She set the fire that drew everyone away from the training areas. Jack, of course, thought you were safely guarded. I caught up to her at her car. She tried to get me with the hypo she injected Glory with. I guess she did that when you two weren't looking.''

She felt like such a fool. Her friend since kindergarten. Why had she not seen how sick she was? What kind of friend was that?

''Julia pointed out the fire,'' she explained. ''Beth thought she should go see what had happened. Then as I was giving Beth a leg up into the saddle, Glory went wild. How did you figure it out?''

''In the note—she must have stuffed it in your purse when she came up behind you in church, by the way—she said you'd worn your mauve outfit for me. Guys just don't say mauve. It was her crucial error. Without it we'd never have known what happened. Even you and Beth didn't know.''

''She'd have been free to try again if you hadn't caught on.''

Jim blinked as if that hadn't occurred to him and she saw the load on his shoulders lighten a little.

''What happens to her now?'' Crystal asked. ''I can't just suddenly not care.''

''She'll be charged with four counts of attempted

murder and a laundry list of lesser charges here for last night's attempt with the bomb and today's. Joe King has the DA of your home county preparing charges on three counts of attempted murder for both attempts on you and the one on me. I'd guess a weapons offense, too.''

"She'll never get out of prison, will she?''

"She may never go to prison. I'm sure her lawyer will plead diminished capacity. And I have to tell you, I think it's true.''

"I'd rather think of her in a mental institution than prison,'' she told him, tears once again spilling from her eyes.

"And that's one of the reasons I love you, sweetheart. Now I think I've hogged you to myself long enough. There's someone here who's anxious to see you.'' He kissed her hand again and was gone before she could recover her wits. Crystal blinked. Had he said he loved her? Was that just a careless figure of speech or had he meant it? And if he did, what did that mean for them?

"Even with the frown you're looking better than the other one,'' Jack said, peeking his head in the door.

Had Beth been hurt after all? "Is Beth hurt?''

"Better than Jim. Man, has he ever got it bad. Talk about being as nervous as a cat in a room full of rocking chairs. I owe him a lot. You, too. There's no telling what might have happened if you hadn't tried to distract Glory. Or to you *and* Beth if Jim hadn't gotten there when he did. I couldn't believe it when I got there and found him trying to face down Glory himself. Dad's grateful, too, of course.''

"Dad? Isn't he still angry about my presence nearly getting Mama's house blown up?"

"Maybe you should ask him about that yourself," Jack said a little loudly, and looked toward the doorway.

Crystal blinked as her father stepped into view. She couldn't believe her eyes. "Dad? You came all this way just to see me?"

"What father wouldn't fly around the world, let alone only four hours away, when his child is injured?" Evan Alton asked.

Our father, Crystal almost said.

Jack sent her a look that said he'd read her mind. "I'll leave you two alone. Save some energy for the cop. I have a feeling he's wearing out the tile in the hall again."

Crystal watched her father glance at Jackson uncertainly as her brother walked out.

"Jackson's changed a lot since coming here," he said. "Probably because of that dragon of a biological mother of his."

Meg Taggert a dragon? Well, she'd promised herself she wouldn't go back to pulling her punches with him. "Meg is a lovely selfless woman. And Jackson is the same person he always was. You just didn't notice. Him. Me. The world outside the Circle A."

He nodded. "And I'm sorry as I can be about that. Jackson leaving held a mirror up to me, and I saw something I never did before. I never meant to become so single-minded about all your mother and grandmother entrusted to me that I forgot the two people I was supposed to be keeping it for. You asked me the night before you came here why I'd had so many meetings in Denver. I've started seeing some-one."

Now Crystal was really surprised. Jim had been right even though he'd been teasing at the time. There *was* someone. Crystal didn't know how she felt about that. Not about there being a woman in his life, but that she'd been the reason he began looking at his life when all Crystal's bowing and scraping hadn't done a thing. "You have a girlfriend?"

Her father's eyes nearly bugged out. "No. There'll never be another woman for me. Your mother owned my heart and always will. I'm going to a psychiatrist. She has me on depression medication and we've talked a lot about…things. I've come to see that the ranch shouldn't have been my focus all these years. It should have been my children."

Crystal supposed that was some progress. For some reason she thought of Meg Taggert, who'd lost the love of her life in Jackson's father not long before her father had lost his wife. Meg had apparently turned her focus outward to others, rarely considering her own needs. Her father had turned his focus com-pletely inward, thinking only of his grief and his need to nurture the first home he'd ever known—the one his wife had given him. Really, neither was right in the extreme they'd chosen.

"And now that I've been working with my psy-chiatrist and I've seen the error of my ways—"

"Have you?" Crystal cut in, then closed her eyes against the increasing ache in her head. "You sent me here because my presence endangered Mama's house. It hasn't been Mama's house for twenty-eight years, Dad."

Her eyes flew open when he picked up her hand. "I'm a clumsy oaf, Cris." Her father grimaced. "I've spent my life with plainspoken men and I guess I don't know how to talk to a lady. Even my own daughter."

"I wasn't aware you knew I was a female. And frankly, I'm tired of trying to be your son."

"How could I not know you're a woman? You're the image of your beautiful mother. Sometimes it hurts just to look at you. And I guess I'm about as sensitive as an old pair of boots for never telling you that.

"I sent you here because I was scared of losing you. You'd have been killed if I hadn't gone home because I felt so guilty for snapping at you. I thought you'd be safer with your brother but I said it all wrong. You were balking at leaving so I pushed. I'm sorry if I hurt you."

"If?"

He sighed, let go and stood. "Did. Okay?" He walked to the end of her bed and turned back, his hands jammed in his back pockets. "I want the opportunity to get to know my daughter and to learn how to talk to her."

She was thirty years old and her life thus far had been all about her father. It was a tempting offer but there were *her* dreams, *her* needs, *her* future to consider. She still wasn't sure if Jim's offhanded mention of love was a figure of speech or a declaration. But even if it didn't mean a future for them, in some way she'd found the home she'd never really had—in the green, green hills of Pennsylvania. In the hustle and bustle of the nearby city and suburbs. She could have it all here. She could find a job, a place to live, board Lady at Laurel Glen.

"I'm not coming back, Dad."

Evan looked thunderstruck.

"And I'm not sure Jackson is, either. He hasn't decided. He has something here that you never gave him. Autonomy. He runs his part of the operation as he sees fit as long as he meets up to Ross's end goals. And Beth has very important work here that he's not sure he wants to take her away from for a lesser position for himself at the Circle A where he won't be happy. So if you want to get to know your children, you just may have to find someone to run the ranch for you for a while. And I'm not sure you can stand to do that."

The look in his eyes must have been the same look that Jesus saw in the eyes of the rich young ruler before he turned away and went back to his former life. Her father stood there poised on the brink. He took a deep breath and Crystal held hers.

"I'll give Seth Stewart a call in the morning. Your brother seems to think highly of him and his little operation. Maybe he'd like to try his hand at managing something bigger for a while."

Crystal could have sworn she saw his eyes twinkle as he turned away, promising to be back in the morning.

Jim stood as Evan Alton left Crystal's room. The man looked a little less sure of himself than he usually did. "I owe you a debt, a gratitude, Jim," he said.

"No, you don't," Jim said out of honesty. "My

motives were purely selfish. I'm in love with your daughter and I'm going to ask her to marry me.''

Crystal's father stared for a long second, then reached out to shake his hand. ''That's nice to hear. I think I could guarantee you'd win if you ran for sheriff.''

Jim shook his head and Evan's hand at the same time. ''Sorry. I have a job and Caleb Hart deserves that one.'' He didn't think Crystal would miss a single thing about Torrence. She hadn't been very happy there. ''If you'll excuse me, I'd like to get back in with Crystal. We still have some things to settle.''

Courtesy of Cole Taggert, who had run an errand of mercy to Jim's mother's house, Jim had his grandmother's engagement ring in his pocket. But first things first. He wanted to give her the flowers and candy he'd run downstairs to buy. It might seem silly but he didn't think a woman should get engaged before she'd ever gotten flowers or candy.

At least not his woman.

He mentally winced, then grinned as he reached for the doorknob. If she knew a thought as chauvinistic as that one had even crossed his mind, she would hit him over the head with his flowers and toss his candy at him a piece at a time.

I love her so much, Lord. Please let her say yes.

''You look happy,'' she said, her gaze straying and brightening when she saw the gifts.

''These are for you. Flowers and candy.'' He put the flowers in her arm, dropped the box in her lap and sat on the bed hip to hip.

She looked adorably uncertain, her fingers tracing the raised letters on the gold box of chocolates. ''I—

I guess I should have tried getting kicked in the head before,'' she said, tilting the flowers up to her nose.

The white bandage buried in her raven hair drew his attention. "Promise never to do it again and I'll bring you a present every Friday night for the rest of your life."

Her eyes grew as big as saucers. "That's a pretty big commitment just to stop someone from taking crazy chances."

He pushed a few stray hairs off her cheek. "Not if you love the person taking the chances more than life itself."

She blinked. "And you do?"

"Oh, yeah." He felt his smile widen. He just couldn't stop grinning like an idiot. "I love you. Have for some time. I was just too afraid to admit it."

She stared. Those big onyx eyes staring into his drew him closer. He leaned forward, carefully cupped her head and kissed her. "I was sort of hoping you'd say something like—" he said against her lips "like likewise.

"Ditto," he whispered, and pressed another kiss against her mouth. "Me, too." A third kiss. "Count me in." Another. "Sign me up." And yet another.

"Shut up," she said, giggling. "Of course, I love you."

He sat up and grinned. "Phew! That's a relief. Glad that's settled. Sorry I had to torture it out of you like that. So you like traditions like flowers and candy?"

She smiled. "A lot."

Yeah, she did. He noticed she was practically crushing the flowers, she was hugging them so tight.

"That's what I want to give you, sweetheart." Jim

reached in his pocket. "Like an engagement ring that's been passed down in my family. And a wedding with my bride in white and her groom—that would be me—in a tux, and the church bells ringing like crazy. You think those traditions sound like you'd like them, too?"

"Yes."

"Yes, you like them? Or yes, you'll marry me?"

"Yes, to both." Her smile was one he'd take out of his memory in the future whenever he needed a lift. But he didn't think he'd need one often because the love they'd found was a love that went beyond trial, tribulations and losses. It was a love beyond everything but happiness.

* * * * *

Dear Reader,

This book began to take shape while I worked on *Silver Lining*. I'd continued to receive letters from readers asking about Jim Lovell, a character in *Never Lie to an Angel*, my second book for Steeple Hill Love Inspired. I have to admit Jim had intrigued me, too, and I'd always wanted to write his story, even though he wasn't always a likable character. During his first appearance, he wasn't a believer and railed against the heroine when she prayed a simple prayer, putting the life of the man she loved—Jim's best friend, Greg—in God's hands.

Even though Jim came to the Lord, he never understood why Angelica had prayed that prayer for Greg. Through his love for Crystal and wanting what is best for her, Jim learns that this simple prayer is the safest prayer of all. God is our Father and God is good. We are safe in His hands. Though we may not always understand what is happening in our lives, He does. Life's little bumps and its big ones are made less painful when we know He is there to offer strength and hope of better days ahead.

I hope you can draw strength and hope from *A Love Beyond*'s message and from the entire LAUREL GLEN series.

God Bless,

Kate Welsh

Love Inspired

PROMISE OF GRACE

BY

BONNIE K. WINN

The only miracle in jilted and injured
Grace Stanton's life was Dr. Noah Brady.
The small-town Texas surgeon could treat her
wounds, but could his healing touch mend her
broken heart and restore her shattered faith?

Don't miss

PROMISE OF GRACE
On sale September 2003

Available at your favorite retail outlet.

ALWAYS IN HER HEART

BY
MARTA PERRY

It was supposed to be a marriage of convenience for the sake of Link Morgan's goddaughter and Annie Gideon's orphaned niece. But former couple Link and Annie found their growing feelings difficult to ignore. Would the in-name-only family they'd created become a real, loving one?

Don't miss

ALWAYS IN HER HEART
On sale September 2003

Available at your favorite retail outlet.